PRAISE FOR ROBERT'S WORK

Move over Elmore

Love the dialogue and the character studies...definitely a blend of Mickey Spillane and Elmore Leonard

~ Amazon reviewer Alex Adamson

5.0 out of 5 stars Do Not Miss This Book!

Chazz is the master. Every story he writes immerses you so deeply in its world, you can barely crawl out when the pages are closed. "Brooklyn in the Mean Time" might just be his best yet. I don't know which parts of the story are reality and which are fiction. Chazz presents a version of himself where it might just be autobiographical. Then again, he may be messing with we readers to up the ante in our suspension of disbelief. Either way, it's an amazing book. I loved every syllable. Chazz ranks among the top tier of our generation's storytellers. Do Not Miss This Book!

~ Amazon review by Alex Kimmell, author of *The Key to Everything*

A unique and engaging novel with a compelling plot and well-drawn, idiosyncratic characters.

~ David Pandolfe, Amazon reviewer

Robert Chazz Chute is a versatile author, with books ranging from zombies, vampires, hit men, the end of the world, robots, dreams and time travel. Each book and series is well written, smart and leaves the reader wanting more.

~ Cavewoman reviews

Another good story from a master storyteller

Once again I got completely sucked in by Robert Chazz

Chute. I could not put this book down once I started it. My only regret is that I got this book in November and waited until now to read it. The story is imaginative, engaging, and really not like anything else I've ever read.

~ Amazon reviewer Deborah630

DIG CHAZZ CHUTE

His writing style makes you part of his thoughts & conversations: you are part of his dimension Dear Reader and will "SWING" his every day. Only in Brooklyn can the 90's thrive and remain true. You can never truly return home after you ran from its hurts and pains, when naturally embedded during formative years are often hard to run from. Yet, the raw perspectives of your past with eyes wide open; does allow you truth and thus clarity. From there, knowing the negatives and going ballz to the walls with a cuppla hail Mary's; Chazz rocked it and lives the life he was meant to live and believed in. HIGHLY RECOMMEND!

~ Amazon reviewer MIKALA RATED

Reviews of *Bigger Than Jesus*

Bigger than Jesus Captured My Imagination and Ran!

I have always liked the detective style books of the films from the 30-50's. This book captures all those best features. While reading the book I felt I was transported into a world that was inhabited by all the people and characters that made up the Humphrey Bogart movies, the Mike Hammer books, and the other gritty pulp fiction that I have always liked but somehow could not fully embrace. What helped me do that was the witty style that Robert Chazz Chute writes. It is funny, humorous, often serious and he speaks in a way that mixes the old style and current cultural references that make every one reading it feel included in the story.

~ Tidal Ashbrn, Amazon reviewer

The writing is just superb.... From beginning to end, this is one top notch crime novel. It is a smooth, easy read.

~ David Wilde, Amazon reviewer

Robert Chazz Chute proves that genre fiction can be inventive and unconventional in its use of language while delivering a suspenseful story.

~ Dream Beast, Amazon reviewer

An Excellent Read

I loved this book. It is well written, fast paced and unusual for a gangster book.

~ M Slott, Amazon reviewer

Bigger Indeed!

Oh wow. What can I say? Mr. Chute pulled me in with his POV and kept the twists coming through the whole book. I found the ending to be delightful and perfect. With comedy throughout and a wonderful cast of characters.

~ Jo Michaels, Amazon reviewer and author of *The Fury*

Excellent, fast paced romp

This book plays out like a Guy Ritchie film. The pacing is frenzied, the plot convoluted yet easy to parse, and the characters larger than life. Half the fun is trying to who's trying to betray who. I would whole-heartedly recommend this novel to action fans and can't wait to grab the author's next work in this series.

~Amazon reviewer Rev357

What a fun ride of a crime thriller!

In a short span of a couple of short stories collections and a few novelettes, Robert Chazz Chute has seriously become one of my favourite authors! You can count on him for well-written stories that pack punch, plot twists, clever dialogue and even some hidden wisdom in their pages.

~ Amazon reviewer johligo

Five Stars
Great treat, fun, unpredictable and gritty.
~ Kindle customer, Amazon reviewer

Love
Suspense, humor, love!
~ Shirleyjack, Amazon reviewer

Genuine characters, full of ups and downs. Intricate plot.
~ Julio Wickham, Amazon reviewer

Good Thriller
Kept my attention. Real page turner could not stop reading till I finished the entire book. Read it in one day.
~ Amazon reviewer A. Alpuche

SOMETIME SOON, SOMEWHERE CLOSE

A COLLECTION OF DARK CRIMES

ROBERT CHAZZ CHUTE

TABLE OF CONTENTS

PUNISHMENT IN PORT GEORGE

*V*ela DiJordanno sat at her kitchen table and waited for the police. The forgotten mug of tea at her elbow cooled as she listened to the rain drum on the roof of her little home. Hers was a small village, not more than a couple of dozen buildings spread along the shore of Port George, Nova Scotia.

Her small house, weathered and beaten by Atlantic winds, was built for two. Now her home would only house one. As the rain intensified, the sound calmed her. As Vela listened to the downpour drum the tin roof, exhaustion set in. Her eyelids grew heavy. Vela fell asleep in her kitchen chair and so did not see the police cruiser turn into her long driveway.

She had called the authorities at nine that morning. The local detachment was in Middleton (motto: Heart of the Valley!) Vela startled awake as the clock chimed ten, just in time to spot the looming figure of an RCMP constable pass by her front window to knock on her door.

Vela's left hip ached as she rose from her chair and made her way to the door. Her right hip had already been replaced. The doctors in Halifax put her on a wait-list to repeat the procedure with her left. Though the square footage of her little house was small, pain can stretch the dimensions of any space.

She opened the door to a tall RCMP officer carrying a black briefcase and a black umbrella. The fierce rain played a quick patter on his umbrella that reminded Vela of the drumming of impatient fingers.

The old woman squinted up at the policeman. She thought he looked vaguely familiar. Perhaps she'd seen him before at a baked bean supper to raise funds for Middleton's volunteer fire department. Or perhaps it had been a fundraiser for the Macdonald Museum in town. It was hard to tell. With their little moustaches, all RCMP officers looked alike to Vela.

"Mrs. Jordanno?"

"DiJordanno," she corrected him. "First name Vela. Shall I spell it?"

He cleared his throat. "I'm Sergeant Evan Coleman. They say rain never hurt a Baptist but shall we take this inside, out of the weather?"

Vela searched her memory. "Coleman. Coleman. Are your people from Barrington Passage?"

"My parents have both passed away but, yes, I still have an uncle who lives there. Uh, may I come in?"

"Certainly, Constable. I'm sorry. I'm a bit flustered this morning."

"Understandable." He removed his hat and shook water from his umbrella as he stepped inside.

"I never saw a cop with a brolly before," Vela mused.

He shrugged. "Maybe not regulation but it makes sense. We've had quite a blow these last few days."

She nodded and gestured for him to follow her into the kitchen. As he sat at the table, she stoked the fire in the wood stove and put the kettle back on. "You drinking tea or coffee, Mr. Coleman?"

"Coffee would be nice, thanks."

"I only have instant."

"Tea, then, please, ma'am."

"Tea it is."

"I understand you called the Coast Guard yesterday morning?" he asked.

"They've been out looking for my husband but it's been such a harsh spring. Weather's bad for searching, they told me," Vela said. "Been twenty-four hours since I called the Coast Guard. Jay went out in his boat the morning before that. I suppose I should file a missing person's report with you fellas, too, but with the Coast Guard on it, there didn't seem much point. Water wings won't do out there."

"Mm-hm. That's fine. The Coast Guard called us. So I have this straight, this is the *third* day since you last saw your husband?"

Vela bobbed her head. "Last saw him the night before, actually. Kissed him goodnight and he must've left the house early."

"Did he tell you where he was headed?"

"Just out to check his traps."

"Lobster?"

"No bunnies out in the bay, Constable. We used to sell lobster but, as Jay says, the squeeze is hardly worth the juice anymore."

"Ma'am?"

"His catch was just for us and, when it's good, for some of the neighbors. Used to be bigger business around here. Jay used to help out with the weir, too, don't you know? Up the road at the turn? That was twenty years ago. The weir was great, gettin' on the hip waders and pulling in the catch with pitchforks. The tourists loved it. Too bad the government stopped the weir licenses. The fish are just about gone now, anyway. They say we all gotta acquire a taste for squids and octopuses 'cuz that's what's takin' over."

"I see." The constable placed his briefcase on the table and opened it.

Vela was surprised to find the case was actually a laptop. "I guess you fellas don't take notes with a pencil and a notebook anymore, eh? It's all on computers now."

"For official reports, I use the computer, yes, ma'am. Recording, too. Mind if I record our conversation for the record?" The question seemed to be rhetorical. Coleman set his phone on the table and hit a little red button to begin the interview. "For these sorts of investigations, I have to do everything stiff and official. Do you mind if I get the usual stuff out of the way?"

"Whatever you need to do," Vela said.

"Very well. I have some questions so I wish to give you the following caution. You need not say anything and can expect no hope from any promise or fear from any threat. Anything you say may be used as evidence. Do you want to call anyone? Do you want a lawyer present?"

"My, that sounds serious."

The policeman shrugged casually. "Procedure."

"Am I being charged with something?"

"I'm only gathering information for a missing person's case at this point. Do you understand your rights as I've explained them to you? Do you want to call someone?"

Vela bristled. "Of course, I understand. I'm old, not dumb. I don't need a lawyer. Ask away. I have nothing to hide."

Vela took her seat at the table across from the policeman. She met his eyes with a steady gaze. Her left eye was clouded by a cataract but her right eye was doing the work of two nicely. "When you call me 'ma'am,' it makes me feel even older than I am. Call me Vela. V-e-l-a. One *l* will do. Two is overkill, I say."

"And your husband — "

"Jason. Jason Frances DiJordanno. It says Julio on his birth certificate but he goes by Jason around here. He was always just Jay to me. Is that too confusing?"

"No, but when you say, 'around here' — "

"Since he immigrated. He's a Canadian citizen."

"From Italy?"

"Boston. I've got his passport around here somewhere if you want — "

"That won't be necessary."

"Jay's people are from Boston. He moved up here in his twenties. Decided to move in 1974 because of the war in Vietnam. It ended in '75 and his draft number never came up, anyway, so technically, he wasn't a draft dodger. He preferred the term, 'a person of conscience.'"

The constable tapped on the laptop keys, taking notes. Vela watched his eyes. She believed she could tell a lot about a person by their eyes. Coleman had the eyes of a predatory bird.

"Your husband's age?"

"Sixty-six, ten years younger than me. My girlfriends said I was robbing the cradle but I always looked better than him so it's all even."

Neighbors along the shore typically talked about the weather for half an hour before they got around to why they showed up at the door. With police matters, Vela thought a more efficient approach was called for. "Have you come to tell me they've found Jay?"

Constable Coleman's gaze flicked up from his screen. "We have not found him, no."

"But?"

The policeman paused and slid the laptop aside for a moment. "I'm afraid I have some worrying news, Vela."

"Yes, yes? Don't leave me in suspense."

"The Coast Guard found your husband's boat adrift this morning. It wasn't far out but between the tide and the storm we've had over the last couple of days — "

"Jay wasn't on the boat, was he?"

"I'm afraid not."

"Well, that's a kick in the you-know-what, isn't it? Not that I'm really surprised. I decided the smart thing to do was to give up hope. I did that yesterday."

"I'm sorry," Coleman said. "The Coast Guard is towing the boat in now. Did your husband often go out for more than a day?"

"Never. Well, not anymore, anyway. As I said, he was just supposed to be checking his traps. Jay hasn't stayed out on the water overnight for years. No need. I have my teacher's pension and Jay's parents left him some money. He said that was the benefit of being an only child."

"So Mr. DiJordanno didn't have any money problems?"

"Money problems? We got the satellite dish to pay for each month. That and the upkeep on the boat and Jay's pickup are our only expenses to speak of. Gas prices as they are, that's not nothin,' but we're comfortable."

Coleman looked around her humble home. "No money issues at all? You're sure?"

"Jay and I never kept anything from each other, Constable. If he was broke, I'd know." Vela nodded toward the wood stove. "Our lot is deep, goes back into the woods. We've got enough trees back there to heat the house for as long as I'm alive. I'm not up to much these days so maybe I'll have to hire someone else to swing the axe and saw it up."

"I see." The policeman's tone was skeptical.

"Talking about money is not something we generally do up here except to complain about taxes. Why do you ask?"

"We're concerned, Vela."

"Of course, you are. Not as much as I am but — "

"I spoke to the Coast Guard over the radio. They tell me there's blood on the boat."

"Fish blood?"

"It's a lot of blood, Vela. And it's in the cabin, as well."

"Oh."

"Is there someone you can call? Maybe some family member who might come over to stay with you?"

Vela waved the suggestion away. "No family left. I only had Jay. We tried but never had children. The only children I had were my kids from the school. Thirty-six years of teaching."

"Got a friend to call?"

"No friends, just Jay. Besides which, the local gossips are already waggin' their chins. Everybody's got their radio tuned so they know I called the Coast Guard. Just thinkin' of everyone being up in my business made me hesitate to call them in the first place. Dinah next-door — "

"That would be your neighbor to the east? Dinah O'Gilvy?"

"The same. That pest ran right over with a shepherd's pie when she heard Jay didn't come back after one day. If it's as bad as you're making it look, I'll be buried in casseroles and apple crumble by the end of the week. When somebody dies, every neighbor up the shore starts cooking and baking. No amount of apple crumble keeps the reaper away."

Coleman pointed to the shelf by the sink. "You've got a radio. Have you been listening for Coast Guard chatter?"

"Shore-to-ship, Jay called that radio. I hardly turn it on anymore. I spend most mornings listening to CBC Radio. We used the two-way when Jay was a commercial fisherman. These last few years we needn't bother with it. He was always home in time for supper."

"So you didn't have it on while he was out on the water?"

Vela shook her head.

"Even with the storm?"

"No storm was gonna kill Jay. He's too stubborn."

"Did your husband have any disputes with anyone around here?"

"Disputes? *Hmph.*" Vela jerked a thumb toward the west wall of the house. "Chuck Morse next door took down his hedge last summer. It was a nice, high hedge. Now we've got no privacy between our properties. Chuck got tired of trimming it and just tore it out. Probably pulled down both our property values by ten grand or so. When some come-from-away comes callin' and puts in their offer, ole Chuck'll feel the burn then."

"Did you and Jay plan to sell your land?"

"Someday when we can't load the stove anymore, maybe. Lotta old German and Dutch couples retiring around here. Could get a pretty penny. They'd tear down the house but the lot is worth something. Those foreigners like the idea of watching the highest tides in the world slide in and out and all that claptrap. They wouldn't like it in the winter around here so we'd have to sell in summer — "

"So no serious disputes at all, then?"

"Nah. We're out here in the back of the beyond at the edge of the world, Constable. Trouble never comes around here. From what I hear, the kids in Middleton and Berwick are keeping you fellas busy with chasing drugs. Used to be, Middleton just had a few town police. Started with one cop for the whole town. Now you've got a whole RCMP detachment down there. It's a town but it's really just a little village isn't it? This ain't Halifax. How do you fellas fill your days?"

"Oh, we keep busy. No matter where you live, if there are people, there's always something bad going on." Coleman pulled his laptop closer and went back to tapping the keys.

"I meant no offense, Constable."

"None taken. You ever go out on the boat, Vela?"

"Not in years. I'm a landlubber."

"So you haven't left the cabin since he left?"

"I don't call my home a cabin."

"Sorry. No offense intended."

"None taken," she replied. "No, I haven't moved. I've just been sitting here thinking how quiet the house is without Jay banging around."

"And everything was fine between you two, Vela?"

"*What?*"

"Just covering all the bases." Coleman appeared apologetic. "For the report, you understand."

"Hunky-dory," she said.

"I've heard there'd been some troubles."

"Why? What did you hear?"

"We have a file, an incident from 2016? There was an investigation but no charges were laid. You were admitted to Soldier's Memorial."

"I wasn't admitted to the hospital," Vela said sharply. "I just needed to be patched up a little. Coupla stitches and bruise on my cheek, all it was."

"Jay hit you?"

"No. That was a misunderstanding."

"What am I misunderstanding, Vela? Help me out here."

"If I wanted to make that stuff anybody's business, I would have."

"I spoke to some of your neighbors," Coleman said.

"You must have been poking around early in the day. I hope you didn't wake them up. They're all retirees 'round here."

"Just some initial inquiries."

"And?"

"Someone told me you and Jay were talking about divorce."

"At our age? Really? Away with ya! I'm north of seventy-five years old. I've got a bum hip and that's the good one. I've got arthritis in my claws. I'm blind in one eye and can hardly see out of the other. Jay's deaf as a post. You think folks our age are up for starting over? When you're this far down the line, you ride the train to the end of the trip and get buried side by side, Constable."

"I see."

Vela watched Coleman's eyes. She saw doubt there. The policeman was looking for a case to crack his boredom. She'd seen the same look in bad boys who sat at the back of the classroom, always out to stir up trouble, as if they had nothing better to do.

The kettle was hot and whistling too loud in the small room. She got up slowly, feeling her knees creak as she limped over to the stove and poured the hot water. She handed the constable the hot mug and dropped in a bag of Red Rose tea. "Milk? I don't have cream. I don't have any sugar. Jay insists on that fake stuff because he's pre-diabetic."

"As is will be fine, I'm sure." He took a sip and nodded his thanks.

"It sounds like you're telling me my Jay went overboard in the storm."

"It does look that way, except for the blood."

"Then why all these awful questions? You're jumpin' around like a fart in a mitten. He must've hit his head. You ever been out on the water? Two trawlers can be out there side by side. One will ride the crest of the wave and the other will dip into the trough and it's like the other boat disappears. Can't even see the top of their radio antennas — "

He cut her off. "I have a few reasons to look into this matter further."

"Do tell."

The constable ticked off his points on his fingers. "One, the question of the history of abuse by your husband. Two, you don't seem that upset, Vela. Three, the Coast Guard officer said there's blood in the wheelhouse. 'A blood trail to the rail,' is how he put it. Four, I've heard you have a temper. You didn't leave your teaching career under the best circumstances. Word is, you slapped a boy. Maybe more than one."

Vela ticked off her points on her bent fingers. "One, I was brought up to believe what happens inside anybody's marriage is their own damn business. Two, I'll keep myself to myself, thank you. I don't owe a show of tears to a stranger. Three, sounds like you're jumping to conclusions. Four, I might have had a temper once upon a time but do you really think me, a little old lady with this worn-out old body, was out on the water with my husband? Tossed him overboard, did I? That'd take a miracle."

"Or maybe a weapon."

"*Pfft!*" She made a go-away gesture with both hands.

"Your skiff is down by your boathouse across the way."

"That little thing? Barely seaworthy and I'd never take it out in a storm."

Coleman continued to tap on his computer. "So you didn't leave with him around dawn, the morning of the storm?"

"Hell, no."

"That's another point against you, Vela."

"Hm?"

"You were seen leaving with Jay the other morning."

"Somebody's got their morning's mixed up."

"But you said you never go out on the water."

"Well, hardly ever."

"That's not the quote I've got. You said you hadn't been out on the bay in years. You called yourself a landlubber." He stared at her and waited. To Vela, the pregnant pause was excruciating.

"It's that bitch Dinah next-door, isn't it? She means well but she's got a big mouth. That woman's only a few years younger than me but she always calls me Mrs. DiJordanno. It's as if she thinks she's young enough to be one of my students. Dinah got that breast surgery a few years ago, the kind with the implants? She thinks because they're big and perky that she's found the Fountain of Youth. I dunno who she thinks she's foolin'. All that big blonde hair is a wig. Looks like a bleached Shih Tzu on Dinah. A much younger woman is out there somewhere goin', 'Where's my wig?'"

"Don't blame your neighbor. She's not the only person I spoke to."

"Whatever. Dinah had cancer after her treatments, her hair came back in too thin. One look at her face and it's clear for anyone to see she'd spent too much time in the sun. She's got enough wind-burn, she needs skin grafts at the burn unit. Damn woman looks like an old wharf rat."

Coleman took another sip of his tea, sat back in his chair and gave the old woman a serious look. "Here's the thing, Vela. I used to work in the city. Big cities are loaded up with cameras everywhere. Bank machines, major intersections … everybody's got a cell phone. Six times out of ten, if someone commits a crime, it's caught on video."

"No cameras out in the bay," Vela said.

"But you've got neighbors and a lot of them are tight with each other. They care for each other more out here, I think. Not much goes on out in the country so people pay more attention to what happens. With nothing much to fill their days, people talk."

"Up in everybody's business and gossiping, you mean."

The policeman shrugged. "I've already caught you in a lie, Vela. Sea widows don't lie for no reason so I have to wonder if you're quite as frail as you seem."

"I'm certainly too old for this nonsense."

Coleman's gaze fell on the array of medicine bottles on the kitchen counter. "I bet there are a bunch of pain pills over there. Are you in pain today because that's how you normally are? Or are you limping around from all the work you did to kill Jay?"

"I never."

"It must have been awfully choppy out there, coming back in that little skiff. Pretty brave of you to risk it, coming home through that storm. The waves were high — "

"You're delusional, Constable."

"That doesn't sound friendly," he said.

"We were friendly," Vela replied. "Then you went crazy."

"How long were you planning it?"

"I don't know what you're talking about."

"You must have told your husband something to get him to tow the skiff. As experienced a fisherman as Jay obviously was, why would he go out the morning of a big blow? He'd have had an eye to the weather."

Vela said nothing.

"Your knife block over there looks full, not one knife missing."

When Vela spoke, there was steel in her tone. "If you've got a point, I'd sure appreciate you getting to it."

"In a crime of passion, a person will grab a knife from the kitchen. When it's planned, they don't. It takes a coldblooded killer to use the carving knife from Thanksgiving on a family member. Not if they are gonna use it in the kitchen for food again — "

"Still don't see your point, Constable."

"One of your neighbors tells me Jay used to hunt pheasants on the North Mountain each fall."

"Used to."

Coleman pointed to the gun rack on the wall. A rifle lay in its place on the rack but the other space for a rifle was empty. "I'm guessing that .30-30 would be fine for deer hunting. There wouldn't be much left of the bird if Jay used it for pheasants. Where's his shotgun, Vela? Or did you toss that in the drink after you shot your husband?"

"You're making noises like you've got me," Vela said.

"Probably do," Coleman mused. "Once the boat is in port and I have a forensics team out from Bedford crawl over it, we'll know more."

"Uh-huh."

"If Jay hit you, if you felt threatened, things could go easier. Given your age, I can see where the Crown and the judge could arrive at a lighter sentence — "

"A lighter sentence?" Vela raised her voice for the first time. "I'm far past my best before date! I'm unlikely to survive a judgment against me if I jaywalked!"

"All I'm saying is, if there were mitigating circumstances — "

"I am not so weak I'd ever let Jay hit me! Not and get away with it."

"Was it for his money, then? If you weren't afraid of him, is it about what you could get for the land? More money for one than there would be for two."

"Mind how you go, Constable. The rain is letting up but the shore road is slippery. I'd hate to hear that your car flipped and mangled you before you died in a fire." She gazed into his eyes as she smiled. "That would be terrible."

Constable Coleman smiled for the first time. "True colors, Vela, true colors. You have a problem with anger. Did they really let you keep your teacher's pension after you slapped those kids around?"

Vela's tone was flat. "Goodbye, sir. I thought you came to notify me and console me. You're a wolf in sheep's clothing, you are. I think I need a lawyer. You better leave so I can find someone to sue you and your whole department."

The cop did not move. "The one thing I don't get yet is, what turned you into a killer? A woman with no criminal record doesn't start killing in her seventies. What set you off at this late date? And what made you risk getting rid of him that way. Out in that storm, you both could have been killed."

Vela stood and pointed a bony finger toward the door. The policeman gathered his gear. She walked behind him as he picked up his umbrella by the front door. The rain had stopped. She said nothing as he returned to his car. "See you again, soon, Vela," he called. "I'll be back as soon as I have the forensics report on the boat. Sorry for your loss."

Sorry for your loss, Vela thought. *The bastard is not talking about the loss of my husband.*

Vela turned and limped back into the house. By time she pulled the .30-30 down from its rack and loaded it, Coleman's cruiser was at the end of the driveway and pulling onto the road. Vela watched him go, suddenly disappointed he did not stay. The cruiser's taillights flared as Coleman hit the bend where the weir used to be.

The policeman would return, she was sure, and next time he'd bring out the handcuffs. "I've got too much arthritis and osteoporosis for this bullshit," Vela said. "I guess my Jay was right. I should have quit while I was ahead."

The air smelled fresh and clean as it always did after a storm. Exposed to salt and wind, the pine trees along the shore pointed their twisted branches inland, turning their backs to the salt water and harsh ocean winds. With the storm over, hooded seals had returned to the rocks at the edge of the low tide.

"I wonder if I'll miss this view or will whatever comes next just be nothing?"

Dinah O'Gilvy poked her head over the fence between her property and Vela's. "Mrs. DiJordanno? Are you okay?"

"Peachy," Vela replied.

"You sure?"

Vela took a deep breath and let out a sigh. Shoulders slumped, she walked over to the fence. Her moccasins squelched in the sodden grass. "Hey, Dinah."

"What's the gun for, Mrs. DiJordanno? Did that cop say something to upset you?"

"Listen carefully, Dinah. The police are going to ask you a lot of questions. I've got the important answers. You're going to have to tell them."

Dinah looked mystified. "What's going on?"

"The first thing I want them to know is that Jay never hit me, not once. He wouldn't dare. I took a hard knock a few years ago but it wasn't Jay. Can you tell them that?"

"Of course! I know Jay wouldn't hit you. He's a gentleman and a gentle man."

"He was so nice because he was covering for me. Also, he was afraid of me. He should have been, too."

"I don't understand."

"You don't have to understand it. Just pass it on. The police think I killed Jay — "

"Oh, no!"

"I did it."

"What?"

"Each fall, I hunted deer hunters. Most times I'd just put

them in my scope and pull the trigger for a dry click. Just to dream about their bloody bodies was usually enough. Sometimes I pulled the trigger and it wasn't a dry click. Jay wanted me to stop but he wasn't brave enough to stop me. He used to love me, you know. Thing is, for my man, fear took the front seat. When fear is doin' the drivin', love, laws and morals have gotta take a back seat."

"I can't believe this!"

"Believe it, Dinah. Jay dumped the bodies in the Bay. The police think Jay was my first murder. I've been killing men off and on since long before we moved here. Whenever a hunter went missing from the North or South Mountain in the last twenty years, that was me. There's eight of them all together, weighted down and feeding the fish in deep water off the Isle Haute."

Dinah shrank back. She would have run if she were up to it. "B-but why?"

"I love deer and their big brown eyes, don't you? They are so beautiful. The world would be a better place if it was just white-tailed deer. They only came to Nova Scotia about a hundred years ago. I love them so much. I think they're the only things I've ever really loved. Sometimes they'd come right up to the back porch and eat apples off our trees."

Dinah stared at Vela, speechless.

"I got a taste for murder early on. My father was a butcher. I hated my father and what he did to animals. I made my father's death look like a suicide. I made it look like he fell into his own bone saw."

"Jesus!"

"Jesus looked away when I did that, I imagine." Vela laughed. "Dad was my first — oh, don't walk away, Dinah! I'm not going to hurt you. Someone has to tell the tale."

"What else is there to say?" Dinah's eyes were wide and her hands shook. She obviously didn't want to know more.

"That one time I got beat up and needed a couple of stitches? I thought the hunter I shot was alone. That was the Freeman brothers, two men from Bridgetown. The moment Clive Freeman stopped hitting me so he could go tend to his brother, I got right back up and shot them both." Vela hefted the rifle. "With this."

Tears slipped down Dinah's cheeks. "Why kill your husband, though?"

"Jay wanted me to stop. He said we'd got too old for adventure. I told him that marriage takes work, you gotta keep it fresh, keep the blood pumpin'."

"Other people's blood," Dinah said.

"Jay didn't want to dump any more bodies over the side. The thing people like you could never understand is, murder is a craving for me. I wanted to go out into the woods one more time and bag another hunter. I always said it was for the deer, but come to think of it, it was always for me."

"You're right, Mrs. DiJordanno. I don't understand."

"Well, you were never the sharpest tool in the shed, anyway, dear. Suffice to say, when the craving hits, I gotta have it. I begged Jay, just one more time."

"What did he say to that?"

Vela smirked. "He said, 'That's what you said last time.' He didn't want me to go back into the woods again. We argued." Vela looked down at the .30-30 in her hands meaningfully. "He lost the argument. I used the shotgun on him. Two in the chest. Damn near killed myself getting him over the rail and the storm almost drowned me on the way back."

"Can I go back inside my house now, Mrs. DiJordanno?"

"Sure, sure, fill your boots. Go call the police. Constable Coleman is on his way back to Middleton, I suppose. By the time he gets back, it'll be up to you to preach my story. Can you do that for me and not skimp on the details?"

"Y-yes."

"Thank you, Dinah. You're a dim bulb, standin' there with your bare face hangin' out. Still and all, I always said you meant well. And thank you for the shepherd's pie. You've always been neighbor-ly." Vela pulled back the bolt on the rifle to check the load before turning back.

"What are you gonna do?" Dinah called after her. "You're not going to hurt yourself, are you?"

"Myself?" Vela laughed merrily. "I'm not going to hurt myself, you silly twit. I'm gonna kill myself."

"What?"

"You heard me. Not before I satisfy the craving one more time, though. I didn't care for Chuck taking out his hedge. He pulled it down and then he said our yard looked like shit. That wasn't neighborly, not at all."

Vela limped across her yard, headed for Chuck Morse's house. "He won't be complainin' about the view anymore, I guaran-damn-tee it!"

Dinah was on the phone with the RCMP when she heard the first shot. Too late, she realized she should have called Chuck Morse to tell him not to open his door to his homicidal neighbor.

A moment later, Dinah heard Vela DiJordanno's last shot.

2

DERAILED IN DETROIT

On a moonless Saturday night in September of 1978, Frederick Chelsea Crowel sat in the driver's seat of his father's car in a dimly lit parking lot. He drummed his fingers on the steering wheel as he watched the back door to a Detroit nightclub called the Crimson Paladin. Impatient to get started, Fred had murder on his mind.

Even from the back of the dark parking lot, he could hear the beat of the music in his chest like the pumping of blood. He couldn't identify the tune that went with that bass beat. Not knowing annoyed him. Fred turned the key to listen to WNIC on the radio instead. "Q 100.3 on your FM dial!" the DJ enthused.

The Bee Gees had a couple of monster hits that summer with *Night Fever* and *Stayin' Alive*. The songs seemed to be on the radio constantly. Fred did not dance but he liked singing along and managed a decent falsetto.

As time dragged on, Fred wasn't sure how he felt about what was to come. Boredom and anxiety competed for supremacy. However, he had decided upon his mission and was determined to see it through. The key was to stay calm, get away clean and to have an alibi.

The clouds were too thick that night for Fred to see the stars. However, he was sure they were aligned in his favor. His horoscope had hinted that the odds were on his side. The morning's newspaper had delivered hopeful news from the powers of the zodiac: *Seize opportunities presented, follow through on something you've been planning a long time.*

Fred had indeed been contemplating murder a very long time. It seemed the universe was bending to accommodate his needs. His parents, for instance, had gone to bed uncharacteristically early. His father Simon and his mother Shirley had watched *Love Boat* and *Fantasy Island* and called it a night.

Fred made sure his parents both saw him in his pajamas before wishing them sweet dreams. Then he closed the door to his room, changed into black corduroy pants and a black turtleneck. He sat on his bed and waited until he heard his father's buzzsaw snore. Fred waited another ten minutes to be sure his parents were settled in for the night. Then he tiptoed downstairs. The car keys dangled on a hook by the front door. Fred took them and slipped out the back door.

His father's car was a deep green Oldsmobile Delta 88, the Royale hardtop sedan. "A beast of a car, more like driving a boat," his father often said.

Fred slid the machine into neutral and let it roll down the driveway. He didn't start the engine until he was in the street. He was careful not to speed. Stealing the car was something he had done before several times. He thought of those few forays as test runs for the main event. Tonight, he was sure, was the night he would be reborn. He had left the house a boy. He was determined to return a man.

His father had served in Korea. Though Simon refused to discuss his time in the military, Fred was sure his father had seen action. That was why his dad refused to sign the parental consent that would have allowed Fred to join the Marines at 17. Simon wouldn't even allow his son to have a gun. Fred was told he would have to wait.

"Go to college or learn a trade," his father advised.

"Life is short, Dad," Fred said. "I can't wait to get it started for real."

"But your life has already started."

"Nah, this isn't life yet, Dad. I'm in the waiting room to Life. I'm bored."

As Andy Gibb sang *Shadow Dancing* on the radio, Fred began talking to himself, excited for his first kill. "I'm beginning to learn my trade tonight, Dad. You should have let me sign up for the Marines. Doesn't matter. I'll make my own fun. I'll launch my own war. Tonight I prove what I'm made of!"

For the umpteenth time that evening, Fred touched the sheath of the knife on his belt. *Maybe I should stab them a whole lot,* Fred thought. *That would look like a crime of passion and throw off the cops. No one will think to look for me, not in a million years.*

The blade was so long he had to shift it far to one side so it hung down his outer thigh instead of allowing it to twist his belt uncomfortably and dig into his hip. The knife had a compass in the weapon's butt. The salesman at the Army Surplus store said it was built for combat but Fred thought it was a hunting knife. The little compass would have made it look like a toy if not for the length of the shiny blade.

The knife was dull when he bought it. Fred sharpened it carefully using oil on a whetstone. At the library, Fred had read that neither water nor oil was necessary to hone a blade. In the field, some soldiers even used spit. He worked the blade until he could cut paper with it effortlessly. Fred liked the feel of the oil, the smooth pass of the steel on the stone. It helped carry the swarf away.

Swarf. A good word. Fred loved it. English was not his favorite subject. He didn't have a favorite subject at school. However, he absolutely loved that he knew a word the smartypants kids did not. Swarf referred to the bits of metal that got sanded away as he sharpened his new knife on the stone. Swarf meant waste created by machining.

I am a machine, Fred thought. *Anyone I turn my mind to will become swarf.*

The rear door to the club banged open and Fred looked up,

searching the shadows around the back of the Crimson Paladin. No one headed toward any of the cars. Next to the staff door, he glimpsed the dim orange glow of a cigarette.

Fred smiled as he twisted the key to turn off the radio, silencing *Undercover Angel* while Alan O'Day was in mid-chorus. His left hand was on the door handle when he spotted the glow of a second cigarette near the first. *Two* smokers had stepped out for some air. That wouldn't do. Fred took a deep breath. Two was too much for his first kill. He would wait for a better opportunity to launch an ambush.

The best hunters are patient, he told himself.

Fred turned the key again and listened as *Undercover Angel* wound down to its conclusion. After the DJ plugged a mattress store that had a sale on waterbeds, Andy Gibb was back in WNIC's lineup with *I Just Want to Be Your Everything.*

Alert for patterns others could not see and messages lesser minds refused to hear, Fred felt encouraged by the songs on the radio. He was an undercover angel. The Angel of Death was still an angel and Fred was definitely undercover, pretending to be an ordinary human. Tonight he would be stayin' alive and shadow dancing with his oh-so-sharp blade. He definitely had the night fever and, to his victim, Fred would be their everything. Fate was using the radio to confirm his horoscope. He was sure he was on the right track.

The thump of the music continued wafting from the Crimson Paladin as the night crawled on. Fred grew impatient as he watched people come and go, mostly in pairs. Three times he spotted a group of four or more enter and leave and, for the most part, the revelers seemed to be having a good time. There were pretty girls and drunken men but no one was alone. No one but Fred.

Mom's a birdwatcher, he thought. *Next time, I'll bring her binoculars.*

It bothered Fred that he had failed to foresee the need. In truth, he thought that by this time he would be in the shower in his parent's basement, peeling off his clothes and watching his victim's blood swirl down the drain.

Fred had planned everything else down to the last detail. He had a bag ready to dump his clothes. He even had a mop and cleaning supplies waiting behind the back door. By dawn, not a trace of blood would be found on the basement floor.

The key, he was sure, was to treat the business of killing like a business. It wasn't personal. Killers who knew their victims tended to get caught. A random murder was nearly impossible to solve. "All else being equal," Fred reminded himself.

In order for all else to be equal, Fred had decided on rules for his killings. The first was that the victim must be alone. There must be no witnesses. If bad luck stepped in to thwart him, no witnesses could be left alive. The getaway had to be clean.

He planned to strike fast, complete his mission and steal from the corpse. Fred would permit himself to keep any cash he stole, but there could be no trophies like a watch or a ring. Those he would throw into the Detroit River. Make it look like a mugging gone wrong and the police would be looking for people who had mugged before. Fred had no criminal record. He'd be safe.

And, of course, he would have to wear gloves.

Gloves!

Fred looked down at his bare hands and cursed. *Right, next time, binocs and a checklist.*

He dug around in the glove compartment. Ironically, the glove compartment held the vehicle's insurance, a flashlight, a utility knife, the Delta 88's instruction manual, an old pack of Hubba Bubba bubblegum but no gloves.

Fred's scalp heated up. He clenched his teeth so hard his jaw hurt. How could he forget his gloves?

But he hadn't. The pair of black driving gloves he had purchased at the Army Surplus store sat on the console beside him. He had been on top of them as he leaned across to search the glove compartment. The mistake was so basic and ridiculous, Fred almost laughed.

"It's your first time," he told himself. "Just first-day-of-school jitters."

As soon as he could release the tension building in his body, Fred was sure he'd be fine. *Draw blood and all will be well,* he thought. *I'll be in control. That's what I need.*

Still sweating, he kept cursing his mistake. Sweaty palms meant fumbling around. One mistake could compound another and spiral him into multiple failures. If the worst happened, Fred promised himself he would never let the police take him alive. He would never spend a night in prison. In the unlikely event some cop got lucky, they'd have to kill him.

"Capture and arrest is for losers," Fred sneered in disgust.

The radio soothed him as he waited and watched. Around two, more people began exiting the club. He'd never been inside a bar but he recognized closing time when he saw it. Some sang, many laughed, a few staggered a little. Couples held each other tight, kissing and speaking close, exchanging intimate words, planning to go home and have sex, Fred supposed.

No easy targets presented themselves. When people walked close by, he sank down out of sight and waited for them to leave. Car engines started up and people drove away.

No matter, Fred thought. *Where there's a bar, there will be waitresses.*

Someone would have to stay behind to count the money and perhaps clean the club. There were only a few cars left in the parking lot. It couldn't be much longer until he found the perfect victim.

I am the hunter. At school, I am invisible. That's a bad thing there. Here, invisibility is my power.

As KC and the Sunshine Band sang *That's the Way (I Like It),* Fred heard the staff door bang open. He peered, squinting to get a better look. Light shone through the open door, illuminating a figure. A woman stood with her back to him. She had long platinum blonde hair. The bright light around her head seemed to form a halo. Someone from inside, a male, spoke to her. The words were indistinct.

Fred could barely breathe. "My undercover angel! That's the way I like it!" As soon as the back door to the Crimson Paladin closed, she would be his.

He hurried to pull his gloves on and almost forgot to switch off the power to the radio before exiting the car. He'd thought ahead, making sure the dome light was off. He was careful not to lock the door to the Delta 88.

I will emerge from the darkness like a puma, undetected until my target's last mortal moment.

Fred covered the ground fairly quietly. Stealth required him to move slower than he expected. The packed dirt beneath his feet did not crunch as stones would. However, the potholes made the ground uneven and he was forced to make his way carefully. It would not do to twist an ankle this close to his victory.

His mind raced as he took in details he hadn't considered. *Maybe next time I shouldn't wear shoes. I'll move silently in bare feet.* His pants made a swishing sound with each step as his thighs rubbed together. *And no corduroys next time!*

The woman was still talking to the man in the club as Fred crouched behind a car, careful to stay out of the cast of the light. The woman's long blonde hair was enticing. For the first time, Fred considered taking a trophy. A lock of hair would be obvious and against the rules but he wanted to preserve this moment somehow.

Someday, when I've graduated to kidnapping, I'll take pictures so I can relive the rush over and over. The thought made Fred smile. Maybe he would save up to get a Polaroid camera and take pictures next time. It wasn't a smart idea. However, now that he was in the moment he understood the dark desire to preserve such milestones. People took pictures at birthdays and weddings. How could murder be any less important?

The door shut. Fred and his intended victim were plunged into darkness. He could not believe his luck as the woman headed for the car he was using for cover.

Carefully, Fred slipped toward the rear of the vehicle and crouched behind the trunk, ready to spring. Only then did he drag the long blade from its home on his hip. As soon as she unlocked and opened her door, Fred planned to jump her. He'd cover her mouth with one hand and drive the knife into her heart. He would strike in silence like the ninjas did in martial arts movies.

But the woman paused.

"Somebody there?"

It wasn't a woman. That was a male voice, deep and rumbly.

Don't panic. Stay put. He has to turn his back to get into the car. Wait for it ... wait for it ...

"I can hear you breathe, man. You're breathin' hard. Get away from my car!"

Fred panicked and ran at the man, blade first as if it were a lance and he a knight on a horse. He screamed as he struck. The man did not run. Instead, he gasped in surprise as the knife slid into his side.

Fred's joy was nearly orgasmic. He had succeeded. He had stabbed his target.

The moment of jubilation passed quickly. One wound in the side does not necessarily a murder make. That moment of discovery was precipitated by a blow. For the first time in his life, Fred got a fist in his face. Surprised, he dropped the knife. Fred was even more surprised when his intended target grabbed him by the hair and began driving his face into the roof of the car.

The pain was excruciating but somehow that wasn't the worst part. It got worse when he heard his right cheekbone crack. At least, he thought that's what that sound was. He became sure upon the next blow when his cheekbone seemed to shift and turn to mush.

But even that wasn't the worst part. Fred's new low came when he begged his intended murder victim to stop.

"You grabbed my hair!" Fred yelled. "That's not fair!"

The man's answer came in the form of another half dozen face smashes. Fred's nose broke and he began to lose teeth. The metallic tang of blood filled his mouth.

A light popped on behind them as the back door to the club yawned open. A man called out, "What the hell is going on out there? Benny, what are you doing to that fat kid? Leave him alone!"

"He stabbed me!"

"*What?*"

"Call the cops!"

Between the pause in the beating and the mention of police, Fred found energy in desperation. He tore away from the man's grip. He lost some hair in the process but that didn't matter now. He had to get away.

Tearing off for the Delta 88, he was glad he'd had the foresight to leave the driver's side door unlocked. With the keys in the ignition, he could be blocks away before anyone could catch him. He might even be home before the cops got around to answering the call from the club.

The blond man was following him but he was merely angry. Fred was scared. Fear fueled his sprint for freedom.

He slipped behind the wheel, slammed the door shut, punched the lock and cranked the ignition. The engine did not roar to life. It made a weak sound as something under the hood turned over.

Then ... nothing.

Through tears, Fred gazed at the dashboard in disbelief. The battery indicator light was on but it was very dim. He was to learn later that his father's mechanic had replaced the battery with an old one. Perhaps it was a mistake. Maybe the mechanic had cheated his father. In any case, the radio that had soothed him through his hours of waiting also killed the old battery. And so, Fred was sure, his father's Delta 88 had murdered him.

The man with long platinum blond hair ran up to his window and pounded on it. He was panting and limping and holding his side but he seemed in no danger of collapsing. *"Got me right through the love handle, you sonofabitch!"*

The blond man was soon joined by two large, muscular men whom Fred assumed were bouncers. One carried a big flashlight. The other carried a baseball bat.

Witnesses, Fred thought. *Living witnesses. And my knife is back there somewhere. And I handled it without gloves before ... and ... and ... doom.*

The stars, the horoscope and the radio had all betrayed him. Fred was caught and he didn't even have the means to kill himself.

Except ... Fred's mind raced. He did have one weapon left. The utility knife he'd found was still in the glove compartment.

In the beam of the flashlight, Fred fumbled for the knife.

"Don't be stupid, kid," the bouncer with the baseball bat said. "It's over. Let it be over."

But it wouldn't be over. It wouldn't ever be over. If he was caught, Fred would forever be labeled as the dumb kid who went crazy one night and got thrown in jail. He was already the fat kid everyone called Flintstone.

Everything hurt and it all hurt too much. Gritting what was left of his teeth, Fred felt the bite of the little razor in the side of his neck. A trickle of blood from his neck joined the gush of blood from his broken nose and ruined mouth.

He burst into fresh tears as he felt the razor's edge at his neck. "I can't live. I can't live with this."

Despite his wound, the blond man grinned and shook his head. "He won't do it."

"I will."

"If you were gonna, you would have done it by now."

The blond man sounded so sure, Fred wanted to cut his own throat out of spite.

"You're not smart enough to come up with any famous last words," his victim said.

Fred stared at them through the glass, seething with hatred. After a moment more, the bouncers broke into derisive laughter.

The first police cruiser arrived, its red, white and blue lights strobing the parking lot. This was Fred's moment of discovery. As the bouncers and his intended victim laughed and mocked him through the window, Fred figured out what he was made of.

Swarf. I am swarf.

Fred placed the utility knife on the dash in disgust. He cried out as he raised his hands in surrender. Fred thought he was a boy who would return home a man. He came close. He was tried as an adult.

Fred Crowel went to prison for a short time and it was just as awful as he expected. However, he lived to endure a long parole and a lot of therapy. His parents almost lost their house paying his legal and medical bills.

The boy graduated a year late. His last year of high school

wasn't as hard as prison but it was just as lonely. Every branch of the military rejected his application to join their ranks. The few people who remember Fred from his youth in Detroit think of him as the kid who went crazy and stabbed somebody one night. They've forgotten that he could play guitar and sang pretty well. They don't even remember his real name. They only know the nickname: Flintstone.

Today, at fifty-eight, Fred is a plumber's assistant in Marion, Illinois. He ended up in a trade just as his father hoped. Fred doesn't like his job but he doesn't hate it, either. Fred's parents died within a month of each other last year. He knew he was not welcome at the funerals so he did not attend. He no longer has any contact with anyone in his family.

Sometimes on moonless September nights, Fred's mind drifts back to that night behind the Crimson Paladin in 1978. He thinks of what he might have become. He tells himself he was an immature boy who got caught up in the moment. Discounting a few bouts of road rage, Fred didn't really have enough of whatever it took. "Never determined enough to make a monster, never lucky or talented enough to be a king," Fred tells himself.

Many fall short of their aspirations. Most people fail to make their wildest dreams come true. With age, Fred Crowel has come to accept that hard truth. He used to hate himself but even burning fury eventually fades if left unstoked.

Except for disco. The Bee Gees, KC and the Sunshine Band and the rest of WNIC's Saturday night lineup nearly killed him. Fred still really hates disco.

3

MERCY IN MARYLAND

*R*uth left the front door unlocked, just as I instructed. I creep in and stand in the open doorway. In case she called someone else in the twenty-two minutes it took me to get here, I wait and listen for a full minute. At the slightest indication this will go sideways, I'm prepared to run through backyards, duck down dark alleys and lose myself in the streets. All's quiet except for coughing from somewhere on the second floor. I close the door behind me and begin to relax.

The house is big and cold. Ruth lives in a pricey neighborhood. She probably only shops at Whole Foods or boutique health food stores. There's no way she'd speak to someone like me unless I was some kind of servant or her Uber driver. Or if she were desperate. Tonight, Ruth is very desperate.

A few lights have been left on so I wander a little at first, taking my time to get some sense of who Ruth Childress really is … or was. At the entrance to the kitchen, I pause to sniff the air. Rotting food odors assault my senses. I am sensitive to smells and abhor uncleanliness and disorder. I move on.

The living room is a mess, too. Scanning the room, I suspect

Ruth has been camped out on the couch and watching television for a long time. Used tissues litter the floor. Empty cartons of Chinese take-out are scattered across the coffee table.

Bookshelves are interesting and instructive so I'm drawn there next. Ruth has several shelves of cookbooks, mostly fad diets. The fattest people have the most books about weight loss. I take off one glove and run a finger across the front of the shelf. Dust. I have to smirk at my supposition being confirmed. Ruth has given up. That fits.

How long has she been depressed? I wonder how many appointments she has had with doctors and therapists. Maybe there's a psychiatrist somewhere in the city who is thinking, "I should follow-up with Mrs. Childress and call her Monday morning."

Monday will be too late. Fortunately, I'm here to help.

I climb the stairs slowly and silently. She's expecting me but it's best if my entrance is a surprise. Ideally, I should appear at the foot of her bed as if materializing out of the air, like an angel.

The bedroom door is ajar. I slip in. One small bedside light burns on her nightstand. Ruth doesn't detect my entrance. She lies in the bed on her side. Her cough is deep and harsh. As expected, her pill bottles sit on the nightstand.

A strong smell hits me hard. It's stomach acid. From where I stand, Ruth is just a lumpy pile of bedclothes. I can't see her face but it is evident she has vomited, probably a lot.

During peak experiences, human senses sharpen. Without looking, she senses my presence. "Hello?"

"Good evening, Ruth," I say as gently as I can manage.

She does not even raise her head to see me. "Rory?"

"Yes. I rushed over, just as I promised."

"Thank you. I'm sorry — "

"Don't apologize to me, Ruth. In times like these, why waste more time for regret? Haven't you regretted enough already?"

"I threw up."

"Do you have more prescription medication?"

"I couldn't swallow them all."

"It happens. Between nerves and rushing, I understand. Shall I fetch you some water?"

She raises a bony arm to show me she has a beverage. It's a half-empty bottle of Dewars. She shakes it. "Got some."

When she lifts up just enough to turn her face toward me, I see Ruth's eyes are red with tears. Some of her dirty blonde hair is matted with puke. Ruth is not what I expected. If not for the vomit, she would be lovely. Were she a few years younger, she might pass for Marilyn Monroe without makeup.

This observation gives me pause. Marilyn was a suicide, too. It depends who you believe. The actress might have been murdered by someone sent by the movie studio. Perhaps it was the FBI or CIA trying to protect President Kennedy from blackmail attempts by foreign governments. It's one of those questions that will never be answered. I hate questions like that.

Despite the smell, I move around to the side of the bed to get a better look at her face. Ruth is not merely thin. Her cheeks are hollow. It's not just the vomit that contributes to the stench. Her breath is thick with rot, too. I recognize that look.

"How long have you been sick, Ruth?"

"All my life." Fresh tears slide from her eyes. She doesn't bother to wipe them away. She's not just drunk. Ruth is utterly exhausted. I feel tired just looking at her.

"Let me rephrase the question. How long have you been vomiting your food on purpose?"

"Off and on over the last year," she admits.

"Did something happen today which made you call me?"

I watch the wheels turns slowly as she tries to find her way out of the fog in her brain. In no rush, I wait. Finally, she formulates an answer. "Nothing new."

"I understand. When things are tough for a long time, awful starts to feel normal and we lose track of time. I've been there."

Ruth musters just enough energy to give me a flash of anger. "You think you understand? *Hmph*. Sure — "

I cut her off. "You're bulimic. Your teeth are rotting. You're worn down. You listen to the news too much and you think your troubles are unique. The bad news is, you're not special, Ruth. It used to be that the highest suicide rates were among the elderly and teens. Now the highest rates of giving up are among white people between 45 and 54. How old are you, Ruth? Fifty? Fifty-one?"

"Forty-eight. I .. I have been struggling for a long time."

"Sad, you mean."

"More than sad."

"Sad, made worse by the expectation that you should never be sad."

"Should I be sad?"

"No, but expecting a constant flow of happiness is unrealistic. Unfortunately, never-ending bliss is what we're all told we should expect. That's what businesses are selling you with every commercial promising miracle cures. All the technology of leisure and travel to exotic destinations are selling you on the idea that you should always be riding high. Reality demands energy, Ruth. Getting ahead and staying there requires work and dealing with other people and maybe a bit of self-hatred."

"I do have self-hatred," she admits.

"It comes from never being satisfied with what you've got." I look around. "Nice house, but it'll never be enough, will it?"

"I feel tied down," she says. "And there are always more bills and —

I've heard enough. I've heard it all before. Perfectionism is at the root of her self-hatred. I don't need to be a $300 an hour shrink to recognize her kind. "There's a lot of friction between you and the world, isn't there, Ruth? Bulimia is not your illness."

"It's not?"

"No. Sticking your fingers down your throat after a delicious meal is a symptom. You aren't sick from a disease per se. You're sick of other people, their demands and their endless expectations. You're sick of trying to fit into other people's opinions of who you should be. You're sick of failing to meet *your* expectations. Isn't that true, Ruth?"

She gives a slight, almost imperceptible nod. Then she begins coughing again. I offer her a tissue from the box beside the bed. I look away and wait patiently for the hacking to settle down. I try to focus on the pretty art on the box of tissues: apple blossoms and an illustration of a whip-poor-will.

As her cough settles, I meet her eyes again and give a small smile. I've practiced that smile in the mirror. I can imitate a happy smile and I've mastered the sly smirk (a quirk on just one side of the mouth). Reassuring smiles are more difficult. I have no one to ask, "Does this smile look reassuring to you? Does it make you feel safe? Like you can trust me?"

I do a lot of solid work but all my good deeds leave me without anyone to ask such questions.

"I don't know how it has come to this," Ruth says.

Here it comes, I think, *the excuses and rationalizations.*

"I was a good student, you know!"

"Grades don't matter in real life, Ruth. All academic institutions keep that fact a secret. It wouldn't serve their cause. A doctor or a lawyer who gets straight Cs gets the same piece of paper as the hard-working straight A student."

"But I worked so hard! I did everything right, or tried to. Mostly, anyway.

"More than most, I'm sure," I tell her. "It's a hard old life, my mother used to say." I look around again and start to feel irritated again. Her bedroom is larger than my apartment. "Even among the privileged, it can be difficult to find a reason to keep going."

As she struggles to sit up, the duvet is pulled back so I can see the carnage. Vomit cakes her nightdress and has pooled on the sheet beside her. My own nausea stirs as I count the pills she has expelled from her digestive tract. Either her suicide attempt isn't serious or she threw up early in the process.

I check out the array of pills on her nightstand. Most of the drugs are antidepressants and anxiolytics. She's been hoarding. I'm surprised to find that not all of her stash is prescription. The little blue, brown and pink pills look like MDMA.

Despite the booze and the pills, her brain fog seems to be lifting. I see more light in her eyes as she asks, "Are the paramedics coming?"

"You didn't call the paramedics, Ruth. You called me."

I begin collecting the pills at her bedside, scooping them all into two pill bottles.

"I don't understand. What's going on, Rory?"

"Ruth, it's all about finding realistic solutions that last. Anything I could say to you tonight would be a tiny bandage on a gaping wound. Pretty words don't fix problems. Action is what matters."

"You're taking my drugs away so I can't kill myself?" Still unsure and teetering on the brink, her tone lands somewhere between disappointment and hope.

"No, Ruth. That's not what's happening at all." I hold out the pills. "You know what they say? If at first you don't succeed …"

Ruth Childress showed some real energy then. I'm pleased to say she broke into raucous laughter. When people truly give up, they often exhibit euphoria. It can be a great relief to put down the heavy burden, to surrender.

But why did Ruth call her brother after she called me? I made the mistake of thinking she was serious.

Her brother must have slipped up the stairs just as quietly as I had. He's a big fellow and, as I am soon to discover, an off-duty policeman. His first question is accusatory, "Who the hell are you?"

"This is Rory," Ruth explains. "He's the nice young man from the suicide hotline."

Who can say what spurs the survival instinct even as we circle the drain? There is no hope and yet we lie to ourselves. I understand what too many people fail to comprehend. The inevitable is coming, anyway. Why make such a big deal out of bringing an early end to misery? Why label my calling a crime?

I have helped several callers to the suicide hotline end the lies they tell themselves. Truth tellers are often vilified. I wish I could make them understand I'm not the villain.

Half of all suicides use firearms. Only about 30% choose asphyxiation. Hanging would not be my first choice. However, as soon as Ruth's brother shoves me in a cell at the county jail, I begin twisting the bed sheet into a serviceable noose.

I leave a note to be found under my lifeless body. No explanations are really necessary. Ruth's suffering will continue without me. I alleviated my suffering by serving as their angel of mercy. I owe nothing to anyone.

I do not apologize or offer groveling excuses. My suicide note is a defiant declaration. The note simply reads: *True to myself.*

4

LIVING IN LONDON

(A PALATE CLEANSER FOR THE INTROVERTS IN THE AUDIENCE)

*M*e, standing in the grocery store aisle, arms full of groceries, and sweating.

A Sobeys employee approaches. "Can I get you a basket or a cart, sir?"

"No, thanks. I'm fine."

"Really?"

"I'm...er...hiding."

"Huh?"

"My wife is in the next aisle over. She has the cart. Shouldn't be too much longer."

He looks at me quizzically as I stay put, still struggling with my armful of popcorn, noodle soup and some other goddamn thing (because Rule of Three for whimsicality, am I right?) I begin to curse softly under my breath.

<Beat>

The Sobeys employee continues to stare at me blankly, the same way I look at quadratic equations.

"She's run into people she knows," I explain. "They're talking."

He regards me, still with a question in his eyes. "So she has the cart — "

"People *she* knows, dude! I don't want to meet strangers! This interaction is excruciating enough and you and I haven't even stumbled through awkward introductions!"

"Ah, I see."

"Cool. Thanks for asking."

Internal monologue: Saints preserve us, I'm going to have to stick a #2 pencil in this pest's carotid if he doesn't return to the deli department and leave me alone.

The Sobeys employee gives me what he imagines is a sympathetic smile. To me, it is a pitying smile.

"I understand," he adds, still not scurrying away.

"Yep! Good! I'm fine. Have a good day!"

And yet he lingers.

"I'm Jerry." He extends a hand into my personal space, not realizing he's put his hand through the bars of my cage and it's feeding time.

"You don't get it, Jerry, but you're gonna."

Jerry screams as the #2 pencil sinks home.

And now I've dropped my groceries. In retrospect, he wasn't offering to shake my hand. He was trying to stop me from dropping the ramen noodle soup.

This is even more awkward now. Clean up on Aisle 3.

5

EDUCATING IN EDMONTON

*E*dwin Pulsifer sat alone in his darkened bedroom on the eighth floor of College Plaza 1. Peering through his window, he waited for the woman on the tenth floor of College Plaza 2 to get ready for bed. She had only moved in recently. That would probably explain the lack of curtains on her bedroom window. Edwin had the internet. He could have satisfied his desires with free porn. However, since seeing the woman from College Plaza 2, he didn't want to watch pornography anymore.

The apartment complex was just a few blocks from the University of Alberta campus. Edwin had graduated from the U of A ten years previously. In the intervening time, he'd become a forensic auditor for the provincial government. He hated Edmonton's winters but he liked living close to the university and couldn't imagine moving. There were so many pretty young girls to ogle.

However, the woman from the tenth floor was different. Edwin had dubbed her "College Plaza 2," but was desperate to know her name. She was a little older than many of the girls around U of A, mid-twenties, maybe. He'd spotted her three weeks previously and was entranced from the moment he saw her.

That's what Edwin called his feeling: entranced. A casual

observer would call it lust. That's what Bob Gentry called it when Edwin confessed to his peeping through her bedroom window.

"Don't do that, man," Bob advised. "Please."

Bob was always a buzzkill, Edwin thought. Worse, Bob was after the same promotion Edwin was gunning for.

Edwin had only told Bob about his nightly vigils because he had no one else to tell. Bob sat one desk away eight hours a day. Edwin was not a social butterfly so, despite their competing job ambitions, Gentry had become his proximity friend. If not for the arrangement of their desks in a small office, they wouldn't have spoken at all.

"You could get in trouble," his coworker warned.

"How am I going to get in trouble? Besides, if she didn't want anyone to look, she'd get curtains."

"As a man, it's your duty to avert your eyes and go look at internet porn."

"Regular porn doesn't do it for me anymore," Edwin said.

"Then go to a strip club and help a lovely woman pay for her student debt. Don't look through windows. That's how serial killers start their careers."

Edwin shrugged off Bob's concerns. "It used to be any glimpse of a woman would do. I'd be done and on with my day. If I watch porn now, it has to be intense but now I also need a story."

"What?"

"Maybe some pageantry, big hats, hot chicks speaking in quatrains."

Bob laughed before he shook his head in disapproval. That annoyed Edwin. Either something was funny or it wasn't. "Don't laugh at my joke and then scold me for it."

"How does peeping at some poor woman across a courtyard tell you a story that gets you off?"

"With her in it, reality is suddenly alluring."

"I'd suggest you try dating, but I'm not sure you're ready for that, man. I wouldn't want to encourage you to inflict yourself on anybody."

"You don't understand," Edwin replied. "Watching a stranger … it was an accident at first. I was just looking out my bedroom window late one night. I'd been drinking and I wasn't feeling great. Then I just happened to look up to see this angel pass in front of her bedroom window in a towel. She must have just come out of the shower. She was drying her hair. Even though she was in the next building over, there was something so intimate about it. College Plaza 2 is so beautiful, she must know it. Maybe she's hoping someone is watching — "

Bob shot him a hard look. "Or maybe you're just a creep. You should consider that. It's a serious variable."

"Before you condemn me, I'll remind you how you ogled the waitress at the Keg."

"I did not."

"Sure you did. Remember? She bent over and I caught you at it."

"Ah. And then you told me all about downblouse porn, which I didn't even know was a thing."

"Admit it. There's something special about accidental, incidental glimpses that's better than a fantasy."

"Nothing incidental or accidental about what you're doing, Ed. You're a stalker."

"Don't be so dramatic."

"What would you call yourself? A peeper? A voyeur?"

Edwin regretted sharing so much with his office mate. He decided against telling Bob that he had indulged in a little low grade stalking. Edwin had, in fact, hung out in front of her building hoping to see College Plaza 2 in daylight. He hung out at the complex's gym, hot tub and the pool hoping she would show up. She did not.

The next day, Edwin got out of his apartment early to claim a chair in the window seat of the coffee shop across the street. He spotted her emerging from College Plaza on his first try. Even better, she made a beeline for the coffee shop.

She was not a tall woman but she rocked a black leather coat Edwin associated with motorcycling. She walked with fast and purposeful steps in her high black boots. They clicked on the tile as she hurried inside to place her coffee order.

College Plaza 2's skin was creamy and flawless. Her straight red hair reached down to her perfect, heart-shaped ass. Her leather attire might even have given her a dangerous air but Edwin couldn't imagine her that way. It was her glasses that softened her image. She wore glasses with thick back rims, a feature Edwin considered both sexy and studious. It was as if she were made for him and him alone.

His first daylight effort to know more about College Plaza 2 was startlingly successful. Not only did he get a good look at her, he learned her first name.

The cafe was busy. Edwin had to strain to hear her speak as she placed her coffee order. She leaned in close when she spoke to the bearded man behind the counter. Her voice was low but the tone was pleasant. He wished he were the bearded man behind the counter. He had an excuse to talk to all the pretty girls on campus, if only for forty seconds at a time.

Edwin was disappointed when she moved down to the end of the bar to await her order. She waited patiently and did not look his way. He wanted desperately for her to gaze into his eyes. He fantasized that their eyes would lock and she would feel something stir. She would recognize the need he felt and give him an inviting smile.

He practiced his introduction in his mind as he waited for College Plaza 2 to look up, for their new lives together to begin. *Hi, I'm Edwin! No. Hello, I'm Ed. Hi … I'm Edwin. I'm Ed and I win.*

Nope!

Sadly, that was all he had. What does one say to a goddess? Come here often? That was so cliche, it wasn't even a joke. When he contemplated what to say upon their initial meeting, his mind went blank. Edwin couldn't very well tell her he'd seen her bare ass and wished she'd spend more time hanging out in front of her bedroom window nude.

Like I do for you, Edwin thought. *When I wait and watch for you, I'm always naked.*

"Natalia! One mocha cappuccino for Natalia on the bar!"

Edwin was elated. College Plaza 2 was no more! *Her name is*

Natalia! Such a lovely name for such a beautiful woman! I wonder if she's Russian. Maybe she's descended from Russian royalty.

The way she carried herself, with such strength and confidence, no remote possibility seemed too outlandish to Edwin. In the safety of his apartment, he had told himself that all he wanted was to put a name to her face. Knowing that little bit of information would fuel his fantasies. Now he was encouraged. He wanted so much more.

He had not planned to follow her, not that first time, at least. Edwin waited and watched from his window seat three more times before he got up the courage to follow Natalia. He decided to cut work to find out where she went each day.

"Cover for me on that Chambers file, please," he told Bob on the phone. "I need to take some personal time this morning."

"You okay, pal?" Bob asked.

I'm not your pal, Edwin thought, and hung up before Bob could ask more questions.

Edwin's curiosity, and his lust, pushed through the boundaries of fear and good sense. He had to know more about the leather-clad goddess. If he could somehow learn her last name, he could stalk her Facebook profile and find out everything about her.

If I knew her interests, I'd have my opening line. With just a little more research, Edwin was sure he'd come up with something clever to say. The key, he was sure, was to come up with an approach that didn't sound like an opening line. He was certain men hit on Natalia every day. He needed to say something unique and funny. If he could make her laugh, the rest, he was sure, would fall into place.

Soon, Natalia, you'll be naked in my bedroom.

Edwin followed Natalia to the LRT. Though she was a head shorter than he, her steps were quick. Even though Edwin kept what he considered a discreet distance, he was panting a little and sweating by the time she boarded the train.

He chose a seat six feet away from hers. He had never been this close. She had bright green eyes and cherry red lipstick. If not for her glasses, he would have assumed she wore tinted contact lenses. Between her flaming red hair and green eyes, Edwin fell into a trance. He couldn't take his eyes off her. He imagined her naked, on top of him, moving with feline grace, riding him and smiling.

Look my way. Look my way. Smile at me, please.

But Natalia was fixated on her phone and did not look up once.

If I were a model, she'd notice me, he thought. *If I could afford a flashier suit or had thicker hair…*

Crushed, Edwin's shoulders slumped and his spine bent under the weight of his disappointment. Stewing in entitlement, a nasty thought began to form. Edwin had been prepared to worship her, to do anything for her. His ardor turned to annoyance and then came a sudden flash of hatred. He wasn't worth noticing. In her world, he did not even exist.

What a stuck-up bitch, Edwin thought. *She couldn't even spare me one look? Couldn't ration out one small smile to a mere mortal? C'mon, bitch. Smile. Just once. Give me something to take with me and cherish when I'm alone tonight and staring at you as you get out of the shower.*

But she gave him nothing. Edwin's fantasy was tarnished.

Natalia exited the LRT at Corona Station. Edwin followed and again struggled to keep up. She only paused a few times to linger in front of shop windows on Jasper Avenue. She got too far ahead of him and somehow he lost her. Natalia had disappeared. Ironically, he was only a couple of blocks from his office building.

Worse, that night, new curtains concealed Edwin's view into Natalia's bedroom. Edwin was furious. He could hardly sleep that night. The next day at the office, Edwin lifted his embargo on Bob and complained.

Bob did not lend a sympathetic ear. "Show's over. Get on with your life, man. Maybe just get a life. Stop being a creep. She doesn't owe you anything."

"There's nothing creepy about it," Edwin whined. "I'm just disappointed. I'm only human."

"I'm not sure. Are you?"

"She works in this area. So what if I tried to give fate a helping hand? I could have run into her on the LRT if we just left for work at the same time — "

"Wait," Bob said. "Your mystery woman works around here? You spoke with her?"

"Not exactly."

Bob did not conceal his disgust. "You *followed* her? At this rate, you're going to get yourself arrested!"

Edwin decided to stop confiding in Bob. He didn't even like Bob. Bob couldn't understand. His hair wasn't thinning. He dated both casually and easily. Fuck Bob.

Edwin did not move on. He didn't seek sexual relief from his internet provider, either. Instead, he kept following Natalia. He told himself infatuation had turned to full-blown obsession but the truth was that anger preoccupied Edwin more than admiration.

Soon she'll notice we're on the same train day after day. Hey, a familiar face, I'll say. And she'll finally give me that goddamn smile. After all this, surely I deserve a smile.

On the Friday of Edwin's fifth week of pursuit, Natalia finally spoke to Edwin. She bestowed her long-sought smile upon him, too. It didn't happen on the LRT or at the cafe across the street from College Plaza. She knocked on his apartment door at ten o'clock at night.

Edwin blurted out a laugh as he peered through the peephole. The goddess had come to his door and was asking to be let in. How could this be? *My persistence has paid off! She found me!*

He took the chain off the door and smiled down at her. "Hello."

"My father taught me something," Natalia replied.

"Huh?"

Edwin glanced down the hallway for a second. A huge uniformed policeman stood in the corridor. He was still looking into the officer's stern face when Natalia attacked.

Mace is prohibited in Canada. Pepper spray, if used to fend off dog attacks, is not against the law. For Natalia's purposes, Edwin Pulsifer was a bad dog.

He got one glimpse of her smile as she blasted a stream of burning liquid into his eyes. Edwin didn't see the knee or the foot that slammed up into his testicles but the explosion of pain was clear enough. Edwin stumbled backward and crumpled to the floor.

He heard the door slam shut and, for a moment, he thought the attack was over. His vision blurred with pepper spray and tears, he managed to get one pained glimpse from his left eye. He heard the *schick* of the steel baton as it extended and locked. Then the blows began to rain down on his head, arms and back.

Natalia asked no questions. She was not interested in his excuses. She didn't want an apology. Only a beating would suffice. When she was done, Edwin was crying and helpless.

Natalia panted from the work of breaking him. "My father taught me that when you have a weapon, you do not warn your enemy."

"I'm not your enemy — "

She kicked him in his left kidney hard. Natalia did not have to tell him to shut up. Edwin had finally learned this was a listening time, not a telling time.

"When you have weapon, you conceal it. Your enemy shouldn't see the knife until it has already cut him."

Then Edwin felt the cold blade. He couldn't see it but he was sure it wasn't the steel baton anymore. It was sharp. If he moved an inch, she could open his throat and he'd bleed to death before she got out the door.

"You must understand, if I even see you at the cafe or on the street again, you won't be seen again. Nod if you understand."

Edwin nodded ever so slightly and felt the bite of the blade at his neck.

"I spotted you following me weeks ago. I've been trying to decide what to do. I talked to my father about you, Mr. Pulsifer. He's the cop in the hall."

Natalia let that knowledge sink in a moment before she continued. "If I scream, he'll be in here in a second and it'll be even worse for you. If he only hears your screams, he'll stay out of it. Scream for me, Mr. Pulsifer."

And Edwin did scream.

Long after she was gone, Edwin managed to crawl to the kitchen. He fumbled for the milk and poured it into his eyes to neutralize the burn of the pepper spray. He wanted to go to the bathroom, to lie in the warm spray of the shower. Instead, he spent the night on the floor, curled up in the fetal position. Everything hurt. His balls ached the most.

Sometime in the early morning hours he supposed he must have fallen asleep. Or perhaps it was the concussion that made him pass out. The sun peeped through the blinds as he finally limped to the bathroom. Getting his clothes off was an arduous journey. Piss, shit and blood soiled his underwear. He peeled off the garment and dropped it in the trash.

He thought he would welcome the warmth of the water but the force of the shower hurt him. He had to steel himself to look in the mirror. His right eye was still blurry. He didn't need perfect vision to know that ugly bruises were blossoming all over his body. He found Tylenol in the medicine cabinet and took three pills.

Somehow, Edwin made it to the bedroom and collapsed on the bed. He could not sleep. Instead, he stared at the ceiling. No cogent thoughts came. There was anger, of course, but shame, as well. He'd been made helpless and he would stay that way. If he sought retribution or any legal remedy, he would have to deal with a furious father who also happened to be a cop.

His wandering thoughts pulled into focus as his cell buzzed. He ignored it, preferring to wallow in misery. But the phone kept buzzing and buzzing. The caller's number was blocked. Whoever it was, they would not give up.

Edwin finally relented. "Hello?" His voice was a tortured rasp.

"Hey, pal."

"Bob?"

"I'm just calling to let you know that Human Resources wants to have a chat with you on Monday morning, in case you didn't get the e-mail yet. There's a memo going around the office and apparently several women are coming forward."

"Human Resources? What?"

"There's a concern around the department about employee safety, particularly among the women on the staff. The guys just don't like you."

"What are you talking about?"

"I recorded our conversations, Ed. That used to be a weird thing, didn't it? *Heh*. We all have recording devices on us at all times."

"I don't — "

"It's called a cell phone, bonehead."

Edwin tried to take a deep breath to calm his nerves but the effort hurt too much. He wondered if Natalia had busted a rib. If so, would a shard of a rib puncture one of his lungs? But Edwin's anger was greater than his fear. "You recorded me?"

"Try to catch up, Ed. Yes, I recorded you. I've been concerned about your behavior and your attitudes, particularly toward women, for a long time. Your men's rights activist incel crap is just pathetic. You're always talking shit about women and what you think they owe you."

"This isn't about that, Bob. You're going to get promoted above me. You've been going for that supervisory job and you're using me, just another step on the ladder, huh?"

"You won't be up for that position," Bob informed him. "You'll probably be out of a job soon. I wish I could feel sorry for you but I don't. All you've got is hate, man."

"I hate you."

"I'm not special. You hate everybody. I want you to understand something. I didn't do it for the promotion. The woman in the next tower in your complex isn't the first you've bothered."

"Bothered? I didn't even talk to her until last night." Edwin chose not to share the fact that she'd literally beaten the shit and piss out of him.

"You follow women. You ogle them. You make unwanted remarks and in the end it's clear you hate them. They can't be sure of your intentions or where these ugly encounters are going. They fear you."

Edwin winced at the headache that had taken up residence behind his eyes. "Apparently, they don't all fear me."

And that's really what I want, Edwin thought. *If I can't have their bodies and their respect, I'd settle for their fear.*

Bob tried to explain, "Recording you and all — "

"Bullshit!" Edwin shouted. It hurt to yell but it felt good to hang up on Bob.

Edwin struggled to sit up from his bed and limped slowly to the window. Naked and afraid, he pulled the cord to raise the blinds to let the sunlight in.

Edmonton on a Saturday morning, he thought. *I wonder how many more Saturdays I'll be staying in this city. I'm going to have to move, to start over.*

All thought was cut short as he looked across the space between his building and College Plaza 2. Natalia's curtains were drawn back. Bob and Natalia waved from her bedroom window. They made a good-looking couple, happy and smiling. Bob hadn't betrayed Edwin for the job promotion, after all.

The beaten man guessed that his pursuit of the red-haired goddess had led Bob to Edwin's dream girl.

"You painted me as the bad guy so you could be her white knight. I gave you the perfect opening for a killer opening line, didn't I? Bob, you are such a bastard."

And so, despite everything Edwin Pulsifer had endured, it cannot be said that he had really learned anything at all.

6

SHAKING CHICAGO

On a bright summer morning in Chicago, Clayton Walter Pigeon sat alone in the window booth of a small diner on East Washington Street, one block from Millennium Park. The blue plate special was printed on a note attached to the laminated menu by a rusty paperclip. The note read: *All-day breakfast for the hungry lumberjack.* The offer was three eggs, potato cakes, bacon, sausage, Texas toast and bottomless coffee. Clay was hungry, but not for the special.

The sun had brought the tourists out early. Clay scanned the sightseers with interest, like a hunter in a blind. Slathering their soft bodies with sunscreen, he supposed many of the newcomers would smell of sweet coconut. Most would head toward the park to take pictures of themselves in front of the city's signature landmark, the Cloud Gate, better known as the Bean. Anonymous in the city's throng, it would be easy for many of these strangers to disappear. Their friends and relatives back home would be mystified.

People disappear all the time, Clay thought. Speaking aloud to himself, he murmured, "As if the city just swallowed them up."

"Sir?"

"Hm?" Clay looked back to find the diner's sole waitress had returned to his table to take his order.

"You know what you want?" she asked.

He looked her up and down. The air smelled of burnt coffee. The waitress' apron was greasy and he noticed dirt under her fingernails. He shook his head slowly. "Just coffee, for now, please and thank you."

She bobbed her head and scurried away. He sensed that his presence made her uncomfortable. He meant her no harm. He craved a tourist with soft skin smelling of suntan lotion.

Clay didn't want to make anyone uncomfortable. The keys to not getting caught and staying alive were the three Ps: precautions, politeness, and planning. Of these, politeness was foremost. It was important to be charming, at least until it wasn't. With a bit of sugar and a smile, even a person of his imposing size could talk his way into any home or hotel room. The key was to sound harmless and to fit in.

Clay sat back and let the sunshine warm him, enjoying the heat and the view of the busy street. Sometime soon, somewhere close, someone new to Chicago would disappear, Clay decided. In any city and town, there might be monsters.

Many desire the thrill of the kill, Clay thought. *Some include torture in their repertoire. I am a chef and I am very hungry. I wonder what my next dish will taste like?*

All human meat tasted like pork but Clay was inspired. A coconut glaze would be delicious.

7

AIMS IN AMES

*I*n a high school in Ames, Iowa, Greg Gibson and Ian Foreman sat outside the principal's office staring at each other. Greg's nose was still bleeding. Ian didn't have a scratch on him.

Greg's mother, Debra Gibson, could be heard berating Principal Terry Casca in his office. "You seem to take a boys-will-be-boys attitude. If these guys were any older, it would be assault. Instead, you call what happened to my son 'getting roughed up!'"

"Ian says your son started it, Mrs. Gibson."

"And you know that's bullshit. He's never even received one detention — "

"The fight happened off of school property," Casca interrupted.

"On their way to school! It's not a fight if one kid beats up another kid. That's a mugging. You saw Greg's nose."

"It's not broken — "

"Not the point! If that was you out there with a bloody nose, would you be splitting hairs and making excuses? I don't feel my son is safe in your school. What are you going to do about that?"

"Mrs. Gibson, please try to see this from my perspective. The school year is over this afternoon," Casca replied. "How about we let this rivalry cool down over the summer and if there's any trouble next year, I assure you I'll be all over it."

"So this bully gets another shot at hurting my son before you'll do anything?" Debra asked. "You've already checked out. I hope your pay gets docked because you're already on your summer vacation, aren't you?"

Ian made a point of leaning forward and staring into his victim's eyes. The bully hit Greg with a smug smile. "You called for Mommy. Pathetic."

Greg could hardly contain his tears.

"They can't do anything to me," Ian said. "You're a pussy, Gibson. Always will be. School's out. Have a great summer."

Debra Gibson burst out through the office door and whirled on Ian. "The principal is going to have a word with you. Don't come near Greg again. Ever. I am not kidding."

"Mrs. Gibson!" Casca called from behind his desk. "It would be best if you leave Mr. Foreman to me."

"Sure, like you'll do anything." Debra held out her hand to Greg. "C'mon."

Without thinking, Greg took his mother's hand. Ian snickered. "Be sure to hold Mommy's hand crossing the street, Greggy."

"Ian Foreman!" Principal Casca bellowed. "Get in here!"

Greg cleared out his locker. He did not return to his homeroom class. He missed the year-end school assembly. He didn't pick up his yearbook. No signatures this year, no "Have a great summer!" from any of his friends. Debra drove him home. He would receive his report card by mail in July.

Once home, Greg holed up in his room and could barely string more than a few mumbled words together for Debra. His father Dave was on the road most of that summer. A long haul trucker trying hard to make ends meet, he came home two weekends out of four.

Upon his return, Debra sent her husband straight to Greg's room. "I don't know how to help him. He won't let me. Please talk to him. Find a way."

Dave knocked on Greg's door.

No answer.

"Greg. You sleeping?"

"No."

Dave opened the door and walked in. His son lay sprawled on the bed. His room was a mess. That was unusual for Greg. Clothes littered the floor and several pizza boxes had been stashed in the corner.

"You better put those boxes in recycling. You're gonna get bugs."

Greg shrugged. He didn't even look up.

"I heard you had a rough end to the school year."

"'Roughed up,' according to Principal Casca. I'd like to see him roughed up, see how he likes it."

"You hurt bad?"

"I thought my nose was broken. It's not. I'm just a bleeder."

"We're worried about you. Your mom tells me you're up all night playing games on the computer and staying in bed all day. Did that punch turn you into a vampire?"

"It wasn't just one punch. He sat on me. I tried to defend myself, to get up. I couldn't."

"I'm sure that wasn't a good feeling."

"You think?"

"So … I get that you need to lick your wounds a bit, but you are going to rebound from this."

"Am I? Or am I going to remember it for the rest of my life? I figured I'd stew over it for at least 50 years. That's what you'd do, isn't it?"

"*Heh.* Probably," Dave admitted. "I'm not the forgiving type but I think you are. We really don't want you to let this thing with this boy become the center of your existence."

"Well … it is. I was looking for a job before the school year was over. There aren't any. If there was summer work, somebody else has it now."

"So what do you want to do?"

"Sleep."

Dave sniffed the air and made a face. "Kinda ripe in here. When's the last time you had a shower, son?"

"I'll have one today."

"Greg, talk to me. Is there more to this?"

"I got beaten up! Isn't that enough? Ian Foreman's got a summer job and I'm here, doing nothing."

"So, again, what do you want to do? With your summer, I mean. You only get so many summers."

Greg let out a bitter laugh. "I guess I want to do nothing."

Dave picked up some discarded clothes from a chair and sat down. "I think you're very focused on the problem. Maybe it would help you more if we considered some solutions. Do you want me to talk to this boy's parents?"

Greg looked his father in the eyes for the first time since he entered the room. "No. That will only make it worse." Greg turned on his side and faced the wall. "Just leave me alone, please."

"You've got a couple of months before you have to go back. What would you say to taking some self-defense classes?"

"So a bunch of guys can beat me up in the hope that one guy won't beat me up? No, thanks."

"What about just working out? If you put a little muscle on — "

"I'm not going to gain enough muscle in a couple of months to make Ian leave me alone come September. I'm a little worried he'll come looking for me before then."

Dave put his head in his hands. "I'm trying to help you, Greg."

"You can't. No one can."

"Your mom is thinking that if the school won't do anything, this might be a matter for the police."

"Are you trying to get me killed?"

"It can't really be that serious, can it? You're a couple of kids. This kind of thing happens all the time, doesn't it?"

"It's serious to me but the cops aren't going to do anything, either. If we were adults … well, kids shouldn't have to put up with this shit, Dad. Adults wouldn't put up with it for a second. If Ian's dad hit you, you'd sue his ass and we'd own their house!"

"Calm down, Greg."

"That's what I'm trying to do. I can't do it. I don't know how." Greg began to shake and burst into tears. Then he couldn't catch his breath. It was his first panic attack.

The next day, Dave and Debra sat on either side of Greg in the waiting room of their doctor's office. Greg, who had neither showered nor shaved in days, did not want to see the family physician. The boy had refused to get in the car until his parents promised to take him out for ice cream after the appointment. His other condition was that he talk to Dr. Kshatriya alone. "I'm too old for you guys to go in with me to hold my hand."

Greg was soon eating a triple scoop of heavenly hash at the nearest ice cream parlor. Debra had a prescription for an antidepressant in her purse.

"What did the doctor say?" Dave asked.

"To look out for suicidal ideation."

His mother paled. "You've never thought about hurting yourself, have you?"

"Not myself, no," Greg replied. "The drugs can do that to you, though. Dr. Kshatriya said it was unlikely. To tell you the truth, I have a lot more confidence in the power of this ice cream. This waffle cone is the first thing I've felt good about since the last day of school."

They filled the prescription on the way home and Greg began his treatment. If Dave and Debra expected their son's mood to lift miraculously, they were disappointed. Greg was still listless and preferred to stay in his room. When Dave got back to work on the road, Greg could barely muster the energy to wave goodbye to his father.

"You're too old to spank," Debra told him, "but if you don't get outside and ride your bike, I'm turning off the modem and taking away your phone."

That tactic was not as effective as Debra thought it would be. Greg took the medication but he still wanted to stay in bed all day. Debra found that the only way to motivate her son was the promise of food. Every chore became a negotiation.

"The stick isn't working so how about some carrots?"

"I hate vegetables," Greg replied.

"Shower and I'll cook up some Yorkshire pudding for dinner. You love that."

"With lots of mashed potatoes and a roast?" Greg asked.

"Pick up your clothes and put them in the washer and I'll do that."

"Can you get that cheesecake, the one you bought last Thanksgiving?"

"If you shave."

"Pick up a bag of chips, too, and I'll shave."

By August, Greg had put on an unhealthy amount of weight.

At least he's showering, Debra thought. *One battle at a time until he gets past this.*

But she was worried. Upon Greg's follow-up appointment, Debra accompanied her son to voice her concerns.

The physician noticed Greg's weight gain right away. "Depression is a tricky thing. Mood disorders can lead to weight gain. The antidepressants can also lead to weight gain."

"Great!" Debra said. "So we're caught in a trap. What do we do?"

"Mom!" Greg said. "You said you just wanted to listen."

Dr. Kshatriya held up a palm as if his hand was a stop sign. "How are you feeling, Gregory? Are you still obsessing over what happened?"

"In my head, Ian Foreman is still on top of me, sitting on me, pinning me down and calling me names. Then he's punching me in the face and laughing while he does it. It's every day. Every hour of every day that I'm awake, Ian's punching me in the face and laughing about it. He made me feel like I was nothing."

With tears in her eyes, Debra reached over and squeezed Greg's hand. "I'm so sorry. You shouldn't have to deal with this. It's worse than I thought. I didn't know…"

Greg shrugged and pulled his hand from his mother's grip.

"Are you spending any time with friends over the summer, Greg? Getting out and having any fun?"

"What friends? What fun?" Greg replied.

"A couple of your friends from school have called," Debra said. "Frank and Taylor even showed up on our front step. You had me send them away." She looked to the doctor. "I've tried to encourage him but he won't socialize at all."

"Mom!"

"It's true. When's the last time you spoke to anyone but me? You'll talk to your Dad when he's home but when he calls in from the road, you can hardly be bothered. Getting a few words out of you is like pulling teeth. That hurts him, Greg. This hurts me. I'm beginning to think I need antidepressants, too."

Kshatriya said nothing for a few moments while he made notes in Greg's chart. When he looked up, he gave a reassuring smile. "Okay, here's what we're going to do. First, more exercise. Exercise has been found to provide many benefits for mood disorders. It might even be better than any drugs I could give you."

Debra's blue eyes widened. "Then why didn't you tell us that first?"

"Because last month, you couldn't even get him out of bed," Kshatriya replied a little too sharply. He cleared his throat and resumed in a calm tone. "Greg, one meal a day should be a salad, okay?"

"I hate salad."

"Gregory, calories in, calories out. This is simple physics. Calories don't care that you don't like salad. Drink more water, too. Weight gain due to this medication is rare so I'm going to suggest we up the dose a tad."

"How much is a tad? Is that safe?" Debra asked.

"Right now, I'm more concerned about Greg's propensity for weight gain."

"His father's side of the family all have that issue."

"We'll weigh you before you go so we can keep an eye on what the scale has to say. Obesity is more of a threat to your long-term health than some schoolyard scuffle."

"Attack," Debra corrected him. "It was an attack."

The doctor gave a slow nod. "I'm sorry. I did not mean to minimize your situation. That's why I'm also going to suggest a referral to a psychotherapist."

Greg put his head in his hands. "I have to see a shrink now? Great. Meanwhile, I saw Ian's Instagram. He got a car for his seventeenth birthday and he's got a new girlfriend. This is a shitty deal."

The doctor touched Greg's shoulder. "I know this is hard. Life is not fair. It's a tough lesson to learn but you will get past this. Give it time."

That was the moment Greg began to suspect that modern medicine might have no real solutions for him.

Dr. Kshatriya wrote a new prescription and told them his secretary would soon call with the name of a therapist. "By the way, the exercise need not be intense. Just get out in the sunshine and walk every day, okay?"

And walk Greg did. Every day he got out of the house and strolled straight to McDonald's. The salads he ate every day at lunch left him hungry. The low prices of fast food allowed Greg to stretch his weekly allowance and fill his gut.

Kshatriya's office eventually called with a referral to a psychologist. However, Greg couldn't get an appointment until late September. As far as Debra and Dave could see, Greg began to do a little better. He ate the salads, went for long walks and showered each day. They didn't know each walk ended in a fast food binge. When he ate candy bars, he disposed of the wrappers before he got home. He left no evidence in the garbage or in his pockets, not even a receipt.

When Dave returned from delivery runs to California and Florida, he noticed Greg had gained even more weight. He had grown an inch taller over the summer, as well. That seemed to mitigate the weight gain somewhat. Not wishing to make his son self-conscious, he didn't mention it. Instead, Dave asked, "How do you feel about going back to school? Starts next week."

"Not good."

"What would you say if I told you it would be okay with us if you went to a different school?"

"Like a do-over?"

"Exactly. Sometimes life is like a shirt with the buttons in the wrong holes. Doesn't matter if you get the other buttons where they're supposed to be. When you need a fresh start, you need a fresh start. How about it?"

"If I do that, Ian will be right."

"Right? How's that?"

"He called me a pussy."

"You're a pussycat, Greg. We love that about you. You're sweet and smart. That kid is an asshole. As your grandmother would say, 'Consider the source.' You shouldn't be giving any weight to what a bully has to say."

"Maybe I shouldn't, but I do. I don't want to get run out of my school. That would feel like I was proving him right about me."

"We're going to talk to Principal Casca again to make sure what happened doesn't get forgotten. We're not going to let this issue fall through the cracks. You know that, right?"

"Leave it alone, Dad. I've been thinking about Ian all summer. I've gotta deal with it on my own. I have to face this without you guys. I know you want to help but you can't."

"You don't have to deal with this alone."

"Thanks, but this is my problem. Don't talk to Casca and I am not going to run away from this."

"Maybe, with the time you two have had apart, things won't be as bad as you think. You got taller over the summer — "

"You think Ian has matured and found Jesus over the last couple of months?"

Dave shrugged. "Okay, maybe that sounds a little silly, but people can change, Greg."

"I don't think anyone changes for the better in such a short time, Dad. I think in a short time, it's more likely people only get worse."

Though Greg had gained more weight since his last doctor's appointment, Dave and Debra took Greg's decision to return to his school as a positive sign.

The prescribed drugs did seem to help Greg get out of bed. He showered and shaved without anyone having to badger him. "The antidepressants are working," they told each other. Even as they asserted that sentiment in hopes of bolstering the other, neither sounded convinced.

But it wasn't the drugs that made the most difference in their son's behavior. Unbeknown to his parents, it was some research on YouTube that gave Greg an idea of how he might return to school without fear.

On the first day of school, Greg slipped out of his house long before dawn. He walked to the home of his tormentor. From watching videos on YouTube, Greg had learned how to jimmy a door with a butter knife. Fortunately, the trick to defeat the lock was not necessary. There was a key under the mat. Greg pulled on latex gloves he'd brought from his father's workshop and opened the door. No alarm sounded.

The Foreman household was silent as Greg crept up the stairs to the second floor. Though he'd passed in front of Ian's house many times on the way to school, he'd never been inside. However, Ian's room was easy to find. His was the only door with a sign. It read: *Keep Out.*

And Greg thought, *I will not.*

Ian Foreman awoke from a deep sleep with a hand clamped over his mouth, a heavy weight on his back and cold metal at his throat. He struggled for a moment but he was pinned fast.

"*Sh,*" Greg ordered. "If you yell, I'll cut your throat and you'll bleed to death in your bed before your parents can even get up to help you. There's no helping you, Ian. Do you understand?"

Reluctant and resigned, Ian nodded and Greg removed his hand from his mouth.

"Gibson."

"That's right, Ian. It's me."

"What do you think you're doing?" Ian had already begun to pant under Greg's weight.

"I need to tell you something," Greg whispered.

"Get off me!"

Ian couldn't see the blade, but he felt cool metal at his throat again.

"I told you to shut up."

Ian craned his neck, trying to escape the weapon. "Okay, okay. I won't yell. Get off me, please. I can barely breathe."

"Good. Maybe that'll help you focus. We don't have much time."

"Much time to do what?" Ian only wore his underwear to bed. His naked back grew hot under Greg's weight. Even his assailant's breath was hot as he whispered in Ian's ear. Not only was it a struggle to breathe, he felt claustrophobic and his panic escalated with each passing second.

"Shut up and listen, Ian. Do you remember when we were little kids on the same soccer team?"

"Yeah."

"We were like, what? Eleven, right?"

Ian nodded.

"I usually played goalie. I only got one goal that summer. The coach made me a forward for a change and there was a breakaway. You passed to me and I got the goal. We high fived. Do you remember that?"

Sweating and unsure, Ian shook his head.

"Too bad. I kind of liked you back then. You treated me like shit when you were showing off to your buddies but sometimes, when we ended up walking home together, I actually thought you could be cool."

Ian's hair was slick with sweat and he tried to move, to gasp for more air. Greg pushed down on him even harder.

"I guess we really are very different people," Greg said. "I was looking for the good in you. I can't seem to find it. You're barely a human at all. If I were to kill you right now, would it be any worse than putting down a rabid dog?"

Tears began to slip down Ian's cheeks and he struggled to breathe. Greg's weight was pressing him into the mattress so hard, all he could manage was shallow little gulps of air. He gasped in order to get out a few pleading words. "I'm sorry. I picked on you and I'm sorry."

"Not as sorry as you're going to be."

"I said I was sorry. Please, let me up!"

"An apology while you're scared isn't gonna do it, Ian. You ruined my summer. You have no idea what I've been doing these last two months — "

"I just gave you a bloody nose, Greg!" He felt the cool metal at his throat again and slipped back into a whisper. "I only gave you a bloody nose."

"It's not about the bloody nose, Ian. You laughed at me and I can't stop hearing it."

Ian grew ever more tired. A hot drop of sweat dripped from the tip of his nose. His pulse pounded in his ears. He could feel his racing heart working hard, beating against his breastbone. It seemed that even his organs were crushed under Greg's weight. "I'm ... sorry. I'm sorry."

"Do you know what positional asphyxiation is, Ian? Babies die from it. Cops have killed people trying to subdue them."

"Please ... don't do this."

In a nearly conversational tone, Greg continued, "Positional asphyxiation is controversial. Some experiments have been conducted. Putting a weight on somebody's back in a lab is different from more than 200 pounds on your back while a cop is arresting you, though, isn't it? And that's just an arrest. I imagine there's quite a bit of panic while someone is trying to decide whether you should live or die. The cops say positional asphyxiation isn't real or the victim has to have some other health problem — "

"Please don't do this!"

"*Sh.*"

To Ian, his attacker was an irresistible force, no more understood than a sudden, unexpected storm. However, Greg finally understood his tormentor. Ian had bullied him and, now that their positions were reversed, Greg got a taste of how utter domination felt. Ian was under his control. Fighting and winning felt fantastic. This was better than antidepressants, better than even the sweetest and saltiest fast food. The scale of their needs were equal. Ian craved oxygen. Greg only wanted this sensation to go on and on.

"Don't worry, Ian. You won't die of positional asphyxiation. I watched other videos I really like, something that isn't so ... passive."

In a panic, Ian raised his voice again. "Help — "

Greg dropped the butter knife on the floor beside the bed and placed his right hand on the side of Ian's neck. Victim no more, Greg slid his hand around Ian's throat to grab his own bicep in one smooth motion. He'd practiced this move in his mind hundreds of times. Between his weight and his grip, his prey was helpless.

"Life is not fair," Greg whispered. "It's a tough lesson to learn but you will get past this. Maybe ... eventually ... I don't really know."

Desperate, Ian tried to throw his head back to headbutt Greg. His attacker's left hand had already cupped the back of Ian's head.

"I first got the idea for this chat from the name of this hold," Greg whispered. "Most people call it a rear naked choke. It's also called a blood choke."

With his forearm secured around Ian's throat, Greg flexed his biceps and pulled his shoulder blades together. "No more blood to your stupid brain."

Ian soon went limp. Greg listened for any movement in the house as he debated how far to take his assault. It was still dark outside. No one had heard Ian's cry.

I could kill you now, Greg thought. *All I have to do is to keep squeezing and wait.*

He almost did just that. But then he remembered his father's words: *You're sweet and smart.*

When he was sure Ian was unconscious, Greg crawled off him and got to work. He grabbed his prey's phone from its charger and unlocked it with Ian's thumbprint.

As Ian began to stir, Greg jumped on top of him again to repeat the blood choke. The second round of unconsciousness gave Greg time to pull the belt from Ian's jeans and to strip his classmate of his underwear. Before his work was complete, Greg was forced to clamp down on Ian neck four times.

"Could leave brain damage," Greg whispered, "but you were broken long before I choked you out."

Disoriented and afraid, Ian Foreman awoke in his bed. For a moment, he told himself he'd suffered a terrible nightmare. He might even have convinced himself of that lie but for two terrible details. His belt was cinched around his neck and he was naked.

Ian struggled to pull the belt from his neck. Coughing and rasping, he called out as he stumbled through twisted bedsheets and fell to the floor. "Mom! *Mom!*"

Greg had already locked the back door and put the key back under the mat when Ian's first screams reached him. He hurried home, disposing of the latex gloves in a garbage can along the way. He returned the butter knife to the utensil drawer in his kitchen.

"Almost home free," he told himself. "And the show is about to begin."

Sweating and jittery, Greg climbed back into bed. He still had forty-five minutes before his alarm clock was to sound. A cop rang his doorbell, beating his alarm by five minutes.

His father was on the road so it was Debra who opened her door to a stern-looking officer. "Hello. Can I help you, Officer?"

"I'm looking for Greg Gibson. Is he home?"

"It's the first day of school. He's still in bed."

"I need to see him," the cop replied. "Now."

The policeman did not knock. When he walked in, he found Greg with his back to the door, seemingly asleep. When the boy turned over, he made a show of rubbing his eyes and looking bewildered. "Wh-what's going on?"

"I understand you've had a beef with a kid at your school. Ian Foreman — "

Debra appeared in the doorway behind the cop. "What about that little shit?"

"Ian was assaulted sometime in the early morning hours today. He's going to be okay but he had quite a scare thrown into him. He's under observation at the hospital."

"Really?" Greg's surprise looked and sounded genuine.

"You say he was assaulted?" Debra smirked. "Are you sure he wasn't just roughed up?"

"His parents are calling it torture," the policeman replied. "I took the boy's statement. Frankly, that's what I'd call it, too."

"What are you bothering my son about this for?"

"Your son — "

"Ian beat the hell out of my son in June. So what? Greg's been here all night."

"You sure about that? I'd like to hear it from him."

Greg fixed the cop with a defiant look. He'd practiced this speech and he was ready. "Officer, all I want to do is go to school, be left alone and to stay away from Ian Foreman. He's mean. He's one of those kids who will end up in jail one day. In the meantime, normal kids have to deal with him. He walks around like he owns the school — "

"Let's discuss this down at the station, son."

"He's not your son, he's mine," Debra said. "And unless you're arresting him, he's not going anywhere. We'll get a lawyer. Greg has nothing to say without one. You woke him up in his own bed, for Christ's sake! Are you seriously thinking of arresting him? That's bullshit and you know it."

"Ian identified your son as his assailant."

Nervous, his voice climbing to a squeak, Greg asked, "Really? How did I break into his house?"

The officer did not reply.

The alarm clock sounded and they all jumped. It was as if the harsh beeping broke a spell. Greg remembered how it felt to use his weight to pin Ian to the bed, to use his arms to choke him out. He felt confident and in control.

"You know what I want, Officer? I want five more minutes of sleep before I get up and get ready for school. Mom? Can I have waffles for breakfast?"

The officer's phone buzzed and he checked it reflexively. "Hold on. It's the victim's family. Get dressed, Greg. I'll speak with you in a minute."

As the officer stepped out of the room, Debra looked at her son. "Are you okay?"

"I will be."

"We'll take care of this. Don't worry."

"I'm not worried," Greg replied. "I didn't do anything wrong."
He believed that, too.

After his mother closed the door, Greg picked up his phone from
his nightstand. After unlocking the device, he pulled up his school's
website to check his class schedule. His parting gift to Ian was
waiting for him.

The school would not open for another hour. It might take at
least that amount of time for the Foreman family to reach a school
official to take down the photos. It would take some time to get the
school board's tech department in gear or to reach Principal Casca.

Until the school could pull down the pictures, any student in the
senior class who accessed the student portal could see the photos of
Ian with his belt around his neck. In each photo, Ian Foreman
appeared to be indulging in autoerotic asphyxiation. Greg had been
careful to make each shot look like a selfie.

Unsuccessfully indulging in autoerotic asphyxiation, Greg thought. *He's
as limp as a little worm.*

He met the cop halfway down the stairs as the officer was
coming back up. Greg put more urgency and surprise in his voice.
"Sir! Sir! I just checked the student portal! It's pictures of Ian! He's
naked!"

The officer nodded. "Posted from his phone, apparently. One of
your classmates called the family. Can I see your phone a moment,
please?"

The cop took his time looking through the phone, checking
texts and emails. He even went through settings to check the loca-
tion services tab. Greg did not object. For his pre-dawn raid, he'd
left his phone behind. It backed his story that he'd been at home all
night.

When the policeman was done, he looked into Greg's eyes.
"Pretty serious goings-on over at your school, huh?"

"Embarrassing and disgusting. Why would Ian do that?"

"I doubt he did, Greg. Are you sure there isn't anything you
want to tell me? Something this serious can really come back to bite
you, you know?"

"Nothing to tell. Ian's an asshole but I don't think he deserves this."

The cop's brow furrowed with sudden doubt. "Did Ian bother ever anyone else? Somebody more scary than you, maybe?"

Debra stepped in. "Bother anyone else? You mean *bully*? *Assault*? *Attack*?"

"Humiliate?" Greg added.

"I'm sure my son wasn't that little bastard's only victim. Why don't you go talk to the principal? Or my son's doctor? Greg's been so wound up since June, he barely comes out of his room."

The cop looked back and forth from mother to son. "Ian did express surprise you came after him. Scared of your own shadow is how he described you. That accurate, Greg?"

Greg had one more play to make. "Have you considered that maybe Ian posted those pics and regretted it? Now he's looking to victimize me some more and shift the blame? Using me as an excuse since he's embarrassed that he perved out?"

That was the end of Greg's encounter with the police.

Dave was on the road, coming back from Boston, when he received the frantic call from his wife. Dave returned home as quickly as he could. He made it back home by the end of Greg's third day at school. He found his son in his room playing video games.

Over the summer, the boy had barely looked up when Dave entered his room. On this day, Greg rose from his desk chair immediately and gave his father a bear hug. "I told Mom you didn't have to come back early, Dad. I'm glad you did, though!"

Dave gave him a skeptical look. His son hadn't given him such an enthusiastic welcome since Greg was a little boy. "You sure I didn't have to come back early? I think maybe it's good I'm here."

"Ian's not at school, Dad! Since his pictures showed up on the student portal, he's hiding out. His family is embarrassed. It's beautiful." Greg sounded elated.

Dave took a seat in the gaming chair and the boy sat on the bed. "You sure you're okay, Greg?"

"Of course."

"Really?"

"Problem solved."

"Your mom is worried about you."

"I don't get why."

"Maybe you fooled the cops and maybe you didn't. I hear the family doesn't want to press charges. They might even move, Greg."

"And what a loss that would be." Greg let out a laugh.

"Was this you?"

"Huh?"

"Your mom isn't sure you had nothing to do with this. It's kidnapping or forcible confinement or some damn thing. I don't know — "

"Does it matter?" Greg spoke with renewed energy, the words coming fast in little machine gun bursts. "It's over! Everything's changed for the better. I don't even feel like I need comfort food anymore. I told Mom to cancel the appointment with the psychologist. Don't need it. Dr. Kshatriya says I have to go off the antidepressants slowly but, really, I feel fine and back to normal. Better than normal."

"We aren't worried about that kid, son. We're worried about you. We're worried about what's normal for you now."

Greg's face fell. "I'm happy. What more do you want?"

"The truth."

"The truth? Sure. I did something to protect myself. I did what no one else could or would do."

Greg confessed everything to his father. Dave listened without comment. He became more and more uncomfortable as his son smiled and laughed as he recounted the worst of what he had done.

When Greg's story wound down, Dave asked, "One question. If you hadn't found that key under the mat, what would you have done? Come home?"

"I would have jimmied the lock. I found out how — "

"Then I'd probably be talking to you through thick glass right now. You realize that, right? Any sign of forced entry and, odds are, your story would have fallen apart. They'd have brought in a forensics team or — "

"I thought it through. When I found that key under the mat, I switched to Plan B."

"What was Plan A, Greg?"

"If I'd so much as chipped some paint around the lock, I would have used the knife on Ian."

"What are you saying?"

"You know what I'm saying."

"You'd have tried to kill him with a butter knife?"

"I'd have gouged his eyes out with the butter knife. Then I would have strangled him until he was dead."

And again, that worrying bright smile. Dave's sweet and smart son's face was marred with a look of euphoric, sadistic pleasure.

"You can't tell the psychologist everything, but you do have to keep that appointment."

Greg shrugged. "Why?"

"Because I've never heard you speak with such confidence. Nothing wrong with confidence, but I'm very concerned about how you got there."

"Dad, I knew I couldn't put on twenty pounds of muscle in a couple of months, but I could put on fat. I used it right. I defended myself."

"I understand what you did and why," Dave admitted. "But understanding a thing and saying it's okay? That's different. You went beyond defending yourself."

"There was a problem. I fixed it." Greg studied his father's face. "You're not going to tell Mom what really happened, are you? That would probably unfix it."

"You and I will never speak about this again. Now I have to go downstairs and lie my face off."

"You don't think she could handle it? She was pretty mad at Ian, too."

"She might handle it better than I can," Dave replied, "but when someone you love confesses to something like this, the fewer people who know, the better. You think this is cool but you've handed me a heavy weight. I'm gonna have to carry that. I'll be carrying it a long time."

"Sorry, Dad. Not for Ian, but for telling you."

"I've never lied to your mother but I'll tell her you're fine, that everything's fine."

"That's the truth, isn't it?"

"I don't think it is, Greg, but I'm not altogether sure anymore."

Ian Foreman did not return to Greg's school. Before the end of September, he transferred to a high school on the other side of town. He never contacted Greg again. No charges were laid against Greg Gibson or anyone else.

Greg graduated from high school with high honors. Academically and socially, his senior year was his best. The next fall, he entered the Criminal Justice Studies program at Iowa State.

That university had also been Ian's first choice. However, Ian decided to go farther afield after learning Greg planned to attend the same school. Ian Foreman is currently still in training to become a dentist at Louisiana State.

Greg graduated first in his class. He then entered the police academy. Today, he is a rookie deputy serving under the Polk County Sheriff's Office in Des Moines.

His training officer reports that Deputy Gibson exhibits much enthusiasm in performing his duties. What Greg's training officer would never write in any record is that Greg has frequently demonstrated great skill in applying dangerous and illegal chokeholds.

AUTHOR'S NOTE

Thank you for reading *Sometime Soon, Somewhere Close*. Authors and their books live and die by reviews. If you enjoy my work, please review the books and spread the happy word. A review need not be long, it helps support my work and allows me to continue writing.

Cheers!

Robert

You'll find links to all my books at
AllThatChazz.com
and more details on the next few pages.

ACKNOWLEDGMENTS

Thanks to J, C & C, as always, and to Gari Strawn of strawnediting.com for her diligent work and ongoing support of my efforts. Thanks to Russ for his beta reads. The fun doesn't come together without you guys.

ABOUT MY CRIME THRILLERS

I write in a variety of genres. If mystery and suspense and lots of gunplay and explosions are your reading pleasure, you may especially enjoy the following killer thrillers.

The Hit Man Series

"I found myself rooting for the guy with the gun and the Armani suit." ~ Armand Rosamilia, author of *Dying Days*

The *Hit Man* books feel like *John Wick* had sex with a bunch of Coen brothers' movies.

Fast-paced and packed with traps and twists, the wide and easy road out of town is always deadly.

Bigger Than Jesus

Jesus (it's pronounced "*Hay-soose*") Diaz is the funny hit man caught in the gears of The Machine. Jesus craves what we all want: the love of a bad woman and bags of cash. The mob wants him dead. To escape New York will take wit and grit. He's got plenty of both.

Fast-paced and packed with traps and twists, the wide and easy road out of town is always deadly.

Higher Than Jesus

Killing a guy on Christmas is bad luck. Jesus Diaz is hunted by the FBI and the mob. He's also failing miserably at group therapy. From the bad streets of Chicago to the White House, secrets are revealed as badasses burn. Arms deals go sideways. Vicodin brings you up. Willow, the glamazon of your dreams, goes down. The stakes crank ever higher. You wanted a life in movies? Your life is a movie but Happily Ever After could prove elusive. Strap in for a deadly new year.

Hollywood Jesus

The unluckiest assassin meets his deadliest opponent yet. Teaming up with a rising star to break up a human trafficking ring, the action gets rough. Jesus is tougher, or at least he'd like to think so. You're going to love Jesus!

Resurrection, A Hit Man Thriller

Jesus Diaz returns in this new killer crime thriller!

The Machine hasn't forgotten Lily Vasquez disappeared with two suitcases of mob money. They're coming after Lily no matter how far she runs. Jesus Diaz hasn't forgotten his ex, either. He'll do anything to protect her.

Follow the trail of blood, mayhem and vigilante justice from England to Miami and back to the Bronx. Packed with fast action and witty dialogue, strap in for a crazy ride that will have you up all night.

∾

The Night Man

What would you do if your father was kidnapped and your high school sweetheart's husband hurt her? What if you can't go to the cops because they're in on it?

After serving his country for years, Ernest "Easy" Jack hoped his family's reputation was forgotten. All he wants to do is train guard dogs. Unfortunately, small towns have long memories. Back from Afghanistan, the wounded warrior's new war has only begun.

Bad people will go hard on Easy. He's badder and harder.

~

Brooklyn in the Mean Time

When a wayward son returns home, uncovering the past could kill his future. Family secrets are murder.

"Sucks you in and refuses to let go! A true master of his craft!" ~ Alex Kimmell, author of *The Key to Everything*

Dangerous men want their money back and Chazz is on the run. When he discovers a side of his father he never knew, big mistakes must be buried if Chazz is to survive. Digging up the old ugly with his brother could get Chazz killed long before a drug lord's hitman shows up to collect.

Bumbling his way through '90s New York, encounter a new kind of psychological crime novel. Funny, dark and compelling, you're in for a great read on a fast ride as soon as you begin *Brooklyn in the Mean Time*.

**All book links can be found at
AllThatChazz.com.**

ABOUT THE AUTHOR

Robert Chazz Chute is a former crime journalist, a speech writer, book doctor and an award-winning writer living in Other London. He writes killer thrillers, suspense and apocalyptic science fiction. To find out more about his books, please visit his author page at AllThatChazz.com and sign up for updates and deals.

*If you love Robert Chazz Chute's work and want even more interaction, join us on the Facebook fan page for more frequent updates and chat.

facebook.com/robert.c.chute

twitter.com/RChazzChute

instagram.com/robertchazzchute

ALSO BY ROBERT CHAZZ CHUTE

~ THE CRIME THRILLERS ~

Bigger Than Jesus, Book 1 of The Hit Man Series

Higher Than Jesus, Book 2 of the Hit Man Series

Hollywood Jesus, Book 3 of the Hit Man Series

Resurrection, A Hit Man Thriller

The Night Man

Brooklyn in the Mean Time

Sometime Soon, Somewhere Close

~

~ DYSTOPIAN & APOCALYPTIC FICTION ~

This Plague of Days, Season 1

This Plague of Days, Season 2

This Plague of Days, Season 3

This Plague of Days, Omnibus Edition

~

AFTER Life INFERNO

AFTER Life PURGATORY

AFTER Life PARADISE

AFTER Life (Box set)

~

Amid Mortal Words

~

Robot Planet, The Complete Series

~

Haunting Lessons, Book 1 of The Dimension War

Death Lessons, Book 2 of The Dimension War

Fierce Lessons, Book 3 of The Dimension War

Dream's Dark Flight, Book 4 of The Dimension War

~

~ TIME TRAVEL ~

Wallflower

~

~ COLLECTIONS ~

Murders Among Dead Trees

Self-help for Stoners

All Empires Fall

~

~ NON-FICTION ~

Do the Thing: The Last Stress-busting Book You'll Ever Need

~

All book links can be found at

AllThatChazz.com.